# Eating Disorders
## OPPOSING VIEWPOINTS®

# Other Books of Related Interest

## OPPOSING VIEWPOINTS SERIES

*Health and Fitness*
*Health Care*
*Mass Media*
*Mental Illness*

## CURRENT CONTROVERSIES SERIES

*Mental Health*

## AT ISSUE SERIES

*Anorexia*

## CONTEMPORARY ISSUES COMPANION SERIES

*Eating Disorders*

# Eating Disorders

## OPPOSING VIEWPOINTS®

Jennifer A. Hurley, *Book Editor*

Bonnie Szumski, *Editorial Director*
Scott Barbour, *Managing Editor*

OPPOSING
VIEWPOINTS®
SERIES

Greenhaven Press, Inc., San Diego, California

Cover photo: Photodisc

Library of Congress Cataloging-in-Publication Data

Eating disorders / Jennifer A. Hurley, book editor.
    p. cm. — (Opposing viewpoints)
    Includes bibliographical references and index.
    ISBN 0-7377-0651-1 (pbk. : alk. paper) —
ISBN 0-7377-0652-X (lib. bdg. : alk. paper)
    1. Eating disorders. I. Hurley, Jennifer A., 1973–   . II. Series.

RC552.E18 E28212  2001
616.85'26—dc21                                                      00-069183
                                                                          CIP

616.85
HLR

Greenhaven Press, Inc., P.O. Box 289009
San Diego, CA 92198-9009

> "Congress shall make no law...abridging the freedom of speech, or of the press."

*First Amendment to the U.S. Constitution*

The basic foundation of our democracy is the First Amendment guarantee of freedom of expression. The Opposing Viewpoints Series is dedicated to the concept of this basic freedom and the idea that it is more important to practice it than to enshrine it.

# Contents

Why Consider Opposing Viewpoints?     9

Introduction     12

**Chapter 1: How Serious Is the Problem of Eating Disorders?**

Chapter Preface     16

1. Eating Disorders Are a Widespread Problem     17
   *Brooke C. Wheeler*

2. The Prevalence of Eating Disorders Is Overstated     21
   *Donald DeMarco*

3. Eating Disorders Are Harmful     25
   *Sarah Klein*

4. Eating Disorders Are Not Necessarily Harmful     31
   *Georgie Binks*

Periodical Bibliography     37

**Chapter 2: Who Is at Risk of Eating Disorders?**

Chapter Preface     39

1. Adolescent Girls Are at Risk of Eating Disorders     40
   *Suzanne Abraham and Derek Llewellyn-Jones*

2. Preteens Are at Risk of Eating Disorders     49
   *Daryn Eller*

3. Adult Women Are at Risk of Eating Disorders     53
   *Leslie Vreeland*

4. Female Athletes Are at Risk of Eating Disorders     59
   *Renée Despres*

5. Men Are at Risk of Eating Disorders     69
   *Suzanne Koudsi*

Periodical Bibliography     75

**Chapter 3: What Causes Eating Disorders?**

Chapter Preface     77

1. The Media Contribute to the Incidence of Eating Disorders     78
   *Ellen Goodman*

2. The Media Do Not Contribute to the Incidence of Eating Disorders 82
*John Casey*

3. Family Attitudes Play a Role in the Development of Eating Disorders 87
*Sharlene Hesse-Biber*

4. Dieting Can Cause Eating Disorders 100
*Carol Emery Normandi and Laurelee Roark*

Periodical Bibliography 112

**Chapter 4: How Should Eating Disorders Be Treated?**

Chapter Preface 114

1. Pharmacological Drugs May Help People with Eating Disorders 115
Medical Sciences Bulletin

2. Psychotherapy May Help People with Eating Disorders 121
*American Psychological Association*

3. Anorexics Need Hospitalization 125
*David France*

4. Some Anorexics Should Be Allowed to Refuse Treatment 133
*Heather Draper*

Periodical Bibliography 139

**Chapter 5: How Can Eating Disorders Be Prevented?**

Chapter Preface 141

1. Educational Programs Can Help Prevent Eating Disorders 142
*Joanna Poppink*

2. Educational Programs May Increase the Incidence of Eating Disorders 146
*Denise Grady*

3. The Government Can Help Prevent Eating Disorders 151
*Lisa Berzins*

4. Parents Can Help Prevent Eating Disorders            158
     *Susan Spaeth Cherry*

Periodical Bibliography                                  162

For Further Discussion                                  163
Organizations to Contact                                165
Bibliography of Books                                   168
Index                                                   170

# Why Consider Opposing Viewpoints?

*"The only way in which a human being can make some
approach to knowing the whole of a subject is by hearing
what can be said about it by persons of every variety of
opinion and studying all modes in which it can be looked
at by every character of mind. No wise man ever acquired
his wisdom in any mode but this."*

John Stuart Mill

In our media-intensive culture it is not difficult to find differing opinions. Thousands of newspapers and magazines
and dozens of radio and television talk shows resound with
differing points of view. The difficulty lies in deciding which
opinion to agree with and which "experts" seem the most
credible. The more inundated we become with differing
opinions and claims, the more essential it is to hone critical
reading and thinking skills to evaluate these ideas. Opposing
Viewpoints books address this problem directly by present-
ing stimulating debates that can be used to enhance and
teach these skills. The varied opinions contained in each
book examine many different aspects of a single issue. While
examining these conveniently edited opposing views, readers
can develop critical thinking skills such as the ability to
compare and contrast authors' credibility, facts, argumenta-
tion styles, use of persuasive techniques, and other stylistic
tools. In short, the Opposing Viewpoints Series is an ideal
way to attain the higher-level thinking and reading skills so
essential in a culture of diverse and contradictory opinions.

In addition to providing a tool for critical thinking, Opposing Viewpoints books challenge readers to question their
own strongly held opinions and assumptions. Most people
form their opinions on the basis of upbringing, peer pressure, and personal, cultural, or professional bias. By reading
carefully balanced opposing views, readers must directly confront new ideas as well as the opinions of those with whom
they disagree. This is not to simplistically argue that every-

one who reads opposing views will—or should—change his or her opinion. Instead, the series enhances readers' understanding of their own views by encouraging confrontation with opposing ideas. Careful examination of others' views can lead to the readers' understanding of the logical inconsistencies in their own opinions, perspective on why they hold an opinion, and the consideration of the possibility that their opinion requires further evaluation.

## Evaluating Other Opinions

To ensure that this type of examination occurs, Opposing Viewpoints books present all types of opinions. Prominent spokespeople on different sides of each issue as well as well-known professionals from many disciplines challenge the reader. An additional goal of the series is to provide a forum for other, less known, or even unpopular viewpoints. The opinion of an ordinary person who has had to make the decision to cut off life support from a terminally ill relative, for example, may be just as valuable and provide just as much insight as a medical ethicist's professional opinion. The editors have two additional purposes in including these less known views. One, the editors encourage readers to respect others' opinions—even when not enhanced by professional credibility. It is only by reading or listening to and objectively evaluating others' ideas that one can determine whether they are worthy of consideration. Two, the inclusion of such viewpoints encourages the important critical thinking skill of objectively evaluating an author's credentials and bias. This evaluation will illuminate an author's reasons for taking a particular stance on an issue and will aid in readers' evaluation of the author's ideas.

It is our hope that these books will give readers a deeper understanding of the issues debated and an appreciation of the complexity of even seemingly simple issues when good and honest people disagree. This awareness is particularly important in a democratic society such as ours in which people enter into public debate to determine the common good. Those with whom one disagrees should not be regarded as enemies but rather as people whose views deserve careful examination and may shed light on one's own.

Thomas Jefferson once said that "difference of opinion leads to inquiry, and inquiry to truth." Jefferson, a broadly educated man, argued that "if a nation expects to be ignorant and free . . . it expects what never was and never will be." As individuals and as a nation, it is imperative that we consider the opinions of others and examine them with skill and discernment. The Opposing Viewpoints Series is intended to help readers achieve this goal.

Greenhaven Press anthologies primarily consist of previously published material taken from a variety of sources, including periodicals, books, scholarly journals, newspapers, government documents, and position papers from private and public organizations. These original sources are often edited for length and to ensure their accessibility for a young adult audience. The anthology editors also change the original titles of these works in order to clearly present the main thesis of each viewpoint and to explicitly indicate the opinion presented in the viewpoint. These alterations are made in consideration of both the reading and comprehension levels of a young adult audience. Every effort is made to ensure that Greenhaven Press accurately reflects the original intent of the authors included in this anthology.

# Introduction

*"[Western society] is still a man's world, in which girls are taught from an early age to be both self-critical and painfully self-conscious. Every day we experience an avalanche of messages telling us that specific women are too fat [or] too thin."*
—Joan Smith, Independent on Sunday, *March 21, 1999*

*"Several twin studies suggest that . . . family susceptibility [to eating disorders] is largely hereditary."*
—Harvard Mental Health Letter, *October 1997*

Fiji, a small island in the South Pacific that has only had electrical power for fifteen years, was almost completely isolated from Western culture until 1998, when the country's one television station began broadcasting Hollywood-produced programs such as "Seinfeld," "ER," and "Melrose Place." Soon afterward, teenage girls on the island—whose traditional culture values large figures over thin ones—began developing behaviors associated with disordered eating, such as induced vomiting and self-starvation. Anne Becker, an anthropologist at Harvard Medical School who has studied the island's eating habits since 1988, reports that, after the advent of U.S. television programs, 74 percent of Fijian teenage girls said that they felt "too big or fat" and 15 percent had vomited to control weight.

In some cases, Fijian girls exhibited the symptoms of a full-blown eating disorder. According to the *DSM-IV*, a manual of mental disorders created by the American Psychological Association, a woman is suffering from anorexia nervosa when her weight is 15 percent below the normal range and she has not menstruated for three months; other physical symptoms include dry skin, brittle nails and hair, lanugo (fine downy hair on the face and body), constipation, anemia, and swollen joints. Bulimia nervosa is defined as two or more episodes of binge eating, followed by induced vomiting or the use of laxatives, every week for at least three months. Those suffering from binge eating disorder also engage in frequent eating binges, but do not use compensatory measures to prevent weight gain.

Eating disorders have confounded clinicians for more than a century, and the debate over what causes these disorders has yet to be resolved. Becker's study demonstrating the link between television and eating disorders in Fiji lends influence to the theory that cultural values are a significant cause. According to many eating disorders specialists, the prevalence of Western media images equating extreme thinness with beauty causes women to feel dissatisfied with their bodies and consequently to engage in dangerous methods of weight loss. Kathryn Putnam Yarborough explains how society's obsession with thinness, transmitted through media images, affects women:

> It is hard not to be affected by the media bombarding us constantly with the message, "Thin is in!" On TV commercials we are told to "lose weight fast" or "exercise for thirty minutes" to have a beautiful body. Magazines displaying thin, attractive women try to convince us that we are not okay until we "slim our thighs." The overriding message is that we need to change something about ourselves in order to be loved or successful. In particular, if we have thin, fit bodies, "our lives will be perfect."

The results of a study conducted by psychologists Eric Stice, Diane Spangler, and W. Stewart Agras, however, suggest that the media may not be a highly influential factor in the development of eating disorders. The researchers provided a fifteen-month subscription to the fashion magazine *Seventeen* to a random sample of thirteen- to seventeen-year-old girls; a control group read no fashion magazines. The findings surprised many: Participants who spent time reading the fashion magazine did not report any increased body dissatisfaction, belief in cultural ideals of thinness, dieting, or negative emotions. Only adolescents who had already exhibited low self-esteem prior to the study felt depressed after exposure to the magazine.

Stice, Spangler, and Agras's study affirms the theory that psychological problems are the underlying cause of eating disorders. According to the findings of an Australian research team, girls who suffer from anxiety and depression are seven times more likely than others to have an eating disorder. Other research demonstrates that women who are overly sensitive to rejection and prone to feelings of irrational guilt and obsessive worry may be at increased risk of developing eating disorders. Thus, as stated by the *Harvard Mental Health Letter*,

> anorexia has been described as one way a girl with this kind of personality may respond to the prospect of sexuality and independence. . . . Fasting restores a sense of order to her life by allowing her to exert control over herself and others. She is proud of her ability to lose weight, and self-imposed rules about food are a substitute for gaining independence.

Although many experts believe that a psychological predisposition to eating disorders is caused by a person's family environment, recent studies documenting the biological basis of many psychological problems has led researchers to investigate a link between genes and eating disorders. Based on her interview of two thousand twins, psychiatrist Cynthia Bulik estimates that bulimia is 83 percent genetically influenced and anorexia is 58 percent genetic. Matt Crenson, an Associated Press reporter, states that "researchers . . . are far from finding an 'eating disorder gene.' In fact, such a gene does not exist. But having some gene—or more likely, some collection of genes—greatly increases a teenage girl's chance of developing an eating disorder."

The theory that eating disorders are hereditary would explain, for example, why eating disorders are found on the Caribbean island of Curacao, where fatness is considered attractive. However, claim some specialists, the theory that eating disorders are a cultural, rather than a biological, phenomenon better explains why eating disorders are increasing among males as media images of men with perfectly sculpted bodies are becoming more widespread. In the following chapters—How Serious Is the Problem of Eating Disorders? Who Is at Risk of Eating Disorders? What Causes Eating Disorders? How Should Eating Disorders Be Prevented? and How Should Eating Disorders Be Treated?—the authors in *Eating Disorders: Opposing Viewpoints* pose contrasting arguments about the causes of eating disorders and offer solutions as to how society can respond to this problem.

# CHAPTER 1

# How Serious Is the Problem of Eating Disorders?

# Chapter Preface

Both clinical research and personal anecdotes confirm that each of the three main eating disorders causes psychological strain and serious health risks. Anorexics are prone to abdominal pain, lethargy, and reduced bone density, and more than ten percent die prematurely due to starvation, suicide, or heart problems. The recurrent vomiting associated with bulimia erodes teeth enamel and can cause fatal damage to the heart, stomach, and esophagus. Binge eating disorder frequently results in obesity, which can lead in turn to health problems such as cardiovascular disease, diabetes, gallbladder disease, and hypertension, among others.

Although almost everyone agrees that eating disorders have destructive potential, not everyone believes that the disorders are as serious as they are portrayed by the media. In fact, some commentators warn that too much focus on eating disorders, particularly anorexia and bulimia, can be dangerous because it draws attention away from a more widespread health problem: obesity. While only 0.5 to 5 percent of Americans experience an eating disorder, more than a third of all Americans are clinically obese. As columnist Geneva Overholser writes in the *Washington Post*, "All the while we've been worrying about too-thin models, . . . Americans have been growing dangerously fat."

According to advocates for eating disorders prevention, however, the problems of obesity and eating disorders are closely related, and not just because binge eating disorder often leads to obesity. Some contend that society's glorification of thinness provokes women to diet, which increases their risk of obesity as well as their likelihood of developing an eating disorder. Professor Judith Rodin of Yale University argues that "dieting is a chief cause of obesity in America" because it slows down the rate at which the body burns calories; consequently, when dieters resume eating normally, they gain weight.

The conflict over which problem—obesity or eating disorders—deserves more of society's concern is briefly discussed in the following chapter. In this chapter, authors provide contrasting opinions on the seriousness of eating disorders.

*"The number of 10- to 14-year-old girls falling prey to anorexia has increased at an accelerated rate each decade since the 1950s."*

# Eating Disorders Are a Widespread Problem

Brooke C. Wheeler

In the following viewpoint, Brooke C. Wheeler contends that the problem of eating disorders—anorexia in particular—has been steadily growing among American women since the 1930s. She maintains that the constant barrage of media images featuring extremely thin models and actresses causes young women of normal weights to think of themselves as fat; consequently, some take drastic measures to lose weight. Wheeler is a writer and the associate editor of *Macworld* online.

As you read, consider the following questions:

1. What age group is developing eating disorders at the fastest rate, as cited by Wheeler?
2. What evidence does the author provide that fashion magazines affect women's self-images?
3. Why is dieting not the solution to America's obesity problem, according to the author?

In one of the most food-abundant countries in the world, more and more young women are starving each year—voluntarily. A Mayo Clinic study incorporating 50 years' worth of data, published in the February 2000 issue of *International Journal of Eating Disorders*, revealed that the rate of anorexia nervosa in American women has been steadily on the rise since the 1930s.

Young women aged 15 to 24 are toppling into the anorexia abyss at the fastest rate—perhaps, say the study's authors, because these are the ages at which women are the most susceptible to social pressures from media and their peers.

Alarmingly, the study also showed that the number of 10- to 14-year-old girls falling prey to anorexia has increased at an accelerated rate each decade since the 1950s.

Anorexia nervosa is an eating disorder characterized by an extreme reluctance to eat, and is considered to be a long-term illness. Unchecked, it can snowball into severe thinness that causes physical damage: amenorrhea (cease of menstruation), heart arrythmia, osteoporosis, kidney failure, and other serious and potentially fatal endocrine and metabolic damage.

## A Public Anti-Fat Creed

The desire to diet now afflicts younger and younger girls, and many studies have pointed the finger at the influence of movies, magazines, and TV. Visual media has been shaping people's self perception for decades. Unfortunately, images young girls see today are often unrealistic: thin, attractive women who are most likely dependent on a combination of good genes, a personal trainer, and many hours a week devoted to exercise and food monitoring.

And women featured in the media keep getting slimmer and slimmer. Witness the examples on display at the January 2000 Golden Globe Awards: Sarah Jessica Parker, Hilary Swank, Angelina Jolie, Lara Flynn Boyle, Gwyneth Paltrow. Ubiquitous fashion models are also notoriously slim: The average American model is 5'10" and 107 pounds.

Women like these, portrayed in media such as magazines, do have a measurable impact on young females' self-images. Girls aged 10 to 18 who read women's fashion magazines are two to three times more likely to diet than girls who steer clear of the fashion glossies, according to a Harvard study released in the March 1999 issue of *Pediatrics*. Almost 70 percent of those girls said that magazine models influenced their idea of the perfect body shape. Even 60 percent of girls who rarely read fashion magazines said they feel that the media influences their notion of what the ideal figure is.

---

## The Message: Thin Is Healthy

In our modern-day Western culture, we are bombarded by advertising and mass media messages that say women must be as thin as the models they see in magazines and on television; thin is healthy; thinness bring happiness, excitement, success, and fulfillment; women must "concentrate" and work hard in order to be thin. Men and women both drive themselves hard, sometimes compulsively, to achieve these ideals, spending hours of time and thousands of dollars. They starve themselves. They exercise for hours at a time. They disregard their need for a normal body weight and a sufficient amount of food to adequately sustain them.

Susan Renes, *Professional Counselor*, August 1997.

---

So what's the result? Girls who are considered to be a healthy weight start thinking of themselves as fat—and may start taking drastic measures to lose weight. A six-year New Jersey study published in the July 1999 *Archives of Pediatric and Adolescent Medicine* revealed that more than 50 percent of Caucasian girls aged 12 to 16 consider themselves overweight—even though these girls fall into the range considered normal for their age and height. Seven out of 10 of these young girls had tried to lose weight at some point.

Results from the Growing Up Today Study published in a November 1999 issue of *Archives of Pediatric and Adolescent Medicine* showed more correlation. The study found that 9- to 14-year-old girls who want to look like women in movies, magazines, or on TV were 30 to 40 percent more likely to purge food after meals by vomiting or taking laxatives.

### What About Obesity?

For decades Americans have been getting simultaneously both fatter and more vulnerable to eating disorders. About 39 million Americans are currently considered obese, meaning at least 30 percent over a government-defined ideal weight for their height. Twenty percent of U.S. healthcare costs go toward treating obesity-related diseases such as heart disease and diabetes, according to the American Obesity Association.

So isn't dieting a good thing if so many Americans are considered overweight? Actually, all this obsession with dieting could be contributing to adult obesity. A study released in the December 1999 *Journal of Consulting and Clinical Psychology* found that teenage girls who are obsessed with restrictive dieting, appetite suppressants, laxatives, and exercise solely for weight loss are 25 to 85 percent more likely to become obese.

There's no obvious fix for these trends, of course. One study estimates that at the current rate, 75 percent of Americans will be obese by the year 2025. And if the rate of eating disorders continues on its steady climb, a significant portion of the population will also be afflicted with anorexia and bulimia, and obsessed with weight-loss methods. The experts say that the best solution for the nation's weight problems is a healthy combination of nutritious eating and regular, moderate exercise. Unfortunately, the evidence—dozens and dozens of studies like these—keep showing that this is far easier said than done.

*"It may be true that more women die each year from complications associated with being over- rather than underweight. But statistics to this effect would not serve to indict the male establishment."*

# The Prevalence of Eating Disorders Is Overstated

Donald DeMarco

In the viewpoint that follows, Donald DeMarco disputes claims made by prominent feminists that approximately 150,000 women die each year of anorexia. A more accurate assessment, he argues, places the approximate number of women who die of anorexia at fifty-four per year. DeMarco contends that feminists exaggerate the problem of eating disorders as a means of supporting their claim that women are the victims of a misogynistic culture that objectifies female bodies. DeMarco is a professor of philosophy at St. Jerome's University in Waterloo, Ontario, Canada, the author of seventeen books, and a member of the American Bioethics Advisory Commission.

As you read, consider the following questions:

1. What do women who study eating disorders hope to demonstrate, as stated by Joan Brumberg and quoted by the author?
2. How does DeMarco support his claim that feminists have overstated the problem of eating disorders?
3. What is the danger of the current "misinformation explosion," as explained by the author?

Reprinted from Donald DeMarco, "Anorexia and the Misinformation Explosion," *Culture Wars*, September 1997. Reprinted with permission from *Culture Wars*.

Approximately 150,000 women die each year in the United States of anorexia! Startling? Shocking? Unbelievable? Implausible? Well, it must be true. Gloria Steinem said so on page 222 of her best-seller, *Revolution Within: A Book of Self-Esteem:* "in this country alone . . . about 150,000 females die of anorexia each year." Besides, Ann Landers, who works with an impressive coterie of experts, also said so in her syndicated column of April 1992: "Every year, 150,000 American women die from complications associated with anorexia and bulimia." Thus, it must be true. And surely no one should question its citation in the preface of a women's studies text, entitled, *The Knowledge Explosion: Generations of Feminist Scholarship.* The startling figure is not only true, thinks Naomi Wolf, but of such magnitude that it fully justifies a powerful indictment against America's (and no doubt, Canada's) misogynistic culture. She asks, indignantly, in her own bestseller, *The Beauty Myth: How Images of Beauty Are Used Against Women,* "How would America react to the mass of self-immolation by hunger of its favorite sons?" Pushing her rhetoric a bit further, she finds the phenomenon of male-initiated anorexia comparable with the Holocaust: "When confronted with a vast number of emaciated bodies starved not by nature but by men, one must notice a certain resemblance."

We find evidence of the same transition from statistics to ideology in Joan Brumberg's book, *Fasting Girls: The Emergence of Anorexia Nervosa as a Modern Disease.* Brumberg, a historian and former director of women's studies at Cornell University, contends that the women who study eating problems "seek to demonstrate that these disorders are an inevitable consequence of a misogynistic society that demeans women . . . by objectifying their bodies."

## Inaccurate Statistics

Despite what the so-called authorities have said, is it really possible that almost three times as many women die each year in the United States of anorexia than the total number of American men who died in the Vietnam War? Brumberg takes her figure from the American Anorexia and Bulimia Association. Yet, that organization insists it was misquoted.

In a 1985 newsletter, the association had referred to 150,000 to 200,000 sufferers (not fatalities) of anorexia. The National Center for Health Statistics has reported 101 deaths from anorexia in 1983 and 67 deaths in 1988. Thomas Dunn, of the Division of Vital Statistics at the National Center for Health Statistics, has reported that in 1991 there were 54 deaths from anorexia nervosa and none from bulimia. To her credit, Naomi Wolf, after being apprised of her error, has instructed her publisher that her statistics on anorexia are not accurate.

---

## Not a Tremendous Problem

Recently there has been much discussion of disordered eating and dysfunctional eating, and such discussion may give the impression that eating disorders are numerous and that they constitute a scourge on adolescent girls and young women in the United States. But, excepting obesity, medically recognized eating disorders basically number only three, and their incidence in the U.S. is not tremendous.

Beth Fontenot, *Priorities for Health*, vol. 11, no. 3, 1999.

---

It may be true that more women die each year from complications associated with being over- rather than underweight. But statistics to this effect would not serve to indict the male establishment. It would be difficult to convince society that men everywhere are pressuring women to be grossly overweight.

## The Current "Misinformation Explosion"

The great danger connected with the current "misinformation explosion" is that it can readily attach itself to an ideology, in this case, a feminist ideology which, in turn, can actually fuel discrimination. People who fight discrimination, even where the discrimination is real and not merely imagined, with false information (or lies), will find that they are advancing the very thing they are trying to end.

Information is omnipresent. It is readily accessible and is available in limitless supply. But one has little of value to say or write if his information has no relation with truth. Truth alone, not mere information, remains the *sine qua non* of education. It is what, in the final analysis, distinguished education from propaganda. Because ideologies are essentially disconnected from reality, their principal means of sustenance and propagation must come through the exploitation of false data. The anorexia issue is hardly proof that contemporary culture is misogynistic.

## The Popular Sport of Male-Bashing

Male-bashing is a popular sport these days, and men are now paying a heavy price for the fabrications that pass for feminist scholarship. There can be little question that men are, to a certain extent, themselves victims of discrimination.

Misinformation, rash judgment, irresponsible rhetoric, and toxic ideology are potent allies. Bernard Nathanson now readily admits that in the 1960's, when he and the National Association for the Repeal of Abortion were fuelling pro-abortion propaganda with lies, that approximately 300 women died each year from criminal abortions, not the 5,000 that they stated in a press release. Yet this calculated lie was a most powerful lever in lifting protection from the unborn.

It may be difficult to get at the truth. The Internet is infested with misstatements of fact, while the Media is more disposed to disseminate fiction than fact. But ideologies, woven as they are, by lies, deceptions, and inaccuracies, in the end, serve no one. They may appear to be self-serving at first, but when the truth finally comes to light, as it inevitably does, given enough time, they are sources of great embarrassment. The truth sets us free; the lie keeps us locked in fear.

*"Some eating disorder-related damage can be reversed . . . but some is permanent and will never be reversed."*

# Eating Disorders Are Harmful

Sarah Klein

Sarah Klein argues in the following viewpoint that women who suffer from (or have suffered from) an eating disorder are at risk of severe long-term health consequences. According to Klein, the damage is severe enough to cause a decreased life expectancy. Klein is a freelance writer and photographer as well as a columnist for the *Metro Times*, the Detroit weekly alternative press.

As you read, consider the following questions:
1. What are the medical consequences of anorexia, as stated by the author?
2. According to the author, why is bulimia potentially more dangerous than anorexia?
3. What does Klein list as the health effects of bulimia?

Reprinted from Sarah Klein, "The Long-Run Implications of Eating Disorders," April 17, 2000, available at www.thestream.com. Reprinted with permission from the author.

It is estimated that 1 to 4 percent of all young women will develop an eating disorder in their lifetime. Most are white and upper middle class, and the onset of the disorder can occur anywhere from early teens to mid-twenties. Recently the American Psychiatric Association estimated that one out of every five women on a college campus demonstrates bulimic tendencies. The disorders can range from a brief flirtation to a long-term, extreme case. A mild case involves a short period of time, or a woman who only engages in the disorder a few times a week. A severe case is marked by hospitalization, and severe health problems due to the disorder.

With the massive amount of women suffering from eating disorders, the question of long-term health implications arises. Everyone knows that a victim of an eating disorder is extremely unwell during the incidence of the disorder, but what about afterwards? For a long time it was assumed that the body would completely return to normal after the purging or starving was stopped. Most institutions and physicians dedicated to the study of eating disorders have traditionally focused on how best to treat the disorder. However, the medical profession is beginning to examine how an eating-disordered woman fares after her recovery, the forerunner being the US Eating Disorder Association.

The following is an examination of the permanent damage that can be incurred from the two most common recognized eating disorders, anorexia nervosa and bulimia nervosa.

## Anorexia Nervosa

Anorexia is distinguished by the refusal to maintain a normal body weight. The longer and more extreme the starvation, the more severe the health repercussions. A North American woman suffering from severe anorexia [has] the same life-span graph as [a] person from an impoverished country; the rate of decline is steeper, and lifespan is shorter than that of a normal North American woman.

The American Medical Association defines critical weight as a minimum required weight for the body to function properly—this is usually 90 percent of the ideal weight. The critical weight for an average-sized 5'5" woman would be approximately 105 pounds. If a woman weighs less than her critical weight for a substantial length of time, several major health problems will occur:

One of the major consequences of anorexia is the cessation of menstrual periods. When a woman stops having menstrual cycles, she loses estrogen, which in turn will cause bone thinning after as little as six months. This can lead to osteoporosis, a condition that is already problematic for women over the age of 50. Former anorectics will have an even greater risk of developing severe fractures, especially as they enter middle age. Hormone replacement is sometimes used to treat anorectics, but it will not help unless the woman retains her minimal critical weight.

Anorexia severely taxes the heart. Malnutrition causes the heart muscles to shrink and weaken, which in turn causes blood pressure to fall. Anorectics often complain of heart palpitations, and have poor circulation. In severe cases, a heart attack will occur, especially if the woman exercises compulsively. Severe cases of anorexia will cause permanent damage to the circulatory system; even after a woman returns to a normal weight, her heart will take many years to return to full-functioning capacity, and may never return at all. Women with only moderate cases of anorexia will usually return to normal health once they gain weight.

Severe thyroid malfunction is common; the metabolism of an anorectic decreases considerably as the body tries desperately to retain weight. Brain size decreases at very low weights, and muscle weakness and cramping occurs. Stomach and digestion problems arise—digestion is hindered and stomach ulcers sometimes occur. Additionally, because of the depression associated with the disorder, anorectics are at a higher risk of suicide.

## Bulimia Nervosa

Bulimia is characterized by episodes of bingeing and purging—through vomiting, laxative use or compulsive exercising. Bulimics often binge on large quantities of food, however it is also common for a bulimic to purge after a small or normal sized meal.

Although both eating disorders are highly detrimental, many medical professionals consider bulimia the more dangerous disorder, for a number of reasons. Bulimics almost always maintain a normal body weight and are extremely secretive about their disorder. Thus, the friends and family members of a bulimic may not even know of her problems until she is already in an extremely advanced stage of the disorder. The purging aspect of bulimia is extremely detrimental to the human body and causes long-lasting damage

## A Former Anorectic Speaks About Her Recovery

I would like to wrap up all loose ends in a bow and say, See? All better now. But the loose ends stare back at me in the mirror. The loose ends are my body, which neither forgives nor forgets: the random halfhearted kicking of my heart, wrinkled and shrunken as an apple rotting on the ground. The scars on my arms, the gray hair, the wrinkles, the friendly bartender who guesses my age, smiling, saying, "Thirty-six?" The ovaries and uterus, soundly asleep. The immune system, trashed. The weekly trips to the doctor for yet another infection, another virus, another cold, another sprain, another battery of tests, another prescription, another weight, another warning. The little yellow morning pills that keep one foot on the squirming anxiety that lives just under my sternum, clutching at my ribs.

The loose ends are the Bad Days: my husband finding a bowl of mush on the kitchen counter, cereal I poured and "forgot" to eat, my husband arguing with me about dinner (No, honey, let's *not* have rice cakes with jelly). The loose ends are the nightmares of hunger and drowning and deserts of ice, the shivering jolt awake, the scattering of cold sweat. They are the constant trips to the mirror, the anxious fingers reading the body like Braille, as if an arrangement of bones might give words and sense to my life. The desperate reaching up from the quicksand of obsession, the clawing my way a little farther out, then falling back. The maddening ambiguity of "progress," the intangible goal of "health."

It does not hit you until later. The fact that you were essentially dead does not register until you begin to come alive. Frostbite does not hurt until it starts to thaw. First it is numb. Then a shock of pain rips through the body. And then, every winter after, it aches.

And every season since is winter, and I do still ache.

Marya Hornbacher, *Wasted*, 1998.

that will remain apparent long after the bulimic ceases purging behavior. Also, up to 20 percent of bulimics suffer from several other addictions related to the impulse-control issues of bulimia; a high percentage of bulimics also abuse drugs and alcohol, live recklessly and are sexually promiscuous. These related factors also effect the lifespan graph of a bulimic; she is more likely to contract a disease due to drug use and sexual promiscuity. Bulimic women are 32 percent more likely to contract a sexually transmitted disease or become pregnant than non-bulimic women. This has a noticeable effect on the bulimic lifespan graph.

Moderate side effects of bulimia include teeth erosion and decay from stomach acids, and swelling of the cheeks, throat and esophagus. Though the swelling disappears when vomiting ceases, the teeth erosion can cause problems later in life, when a woman's teeth begin to weaken anyway. Most severe bulimics need to get their teeth capped at some point in life.

Vomiting is the most dangerous behavior of a bulimic, because it causes an electrolyte imbalance, which reduces the body's levels of potassium. In the short run, this can cause muscle weakness and spasms, but in the long run it can cause a fatal heart attack. Potassium loss is increased with the abuse of laxatives and diuretics. Some bulimics use syrup of ipecac, a medication that induces vomiting. This medication is carcinogenic if used repeatedly, and can cause sudden death or accidental poisoning.

When purging behavior ceases, the body of a bulimic woman will take a very long time to recover. Bulimics are at a high risk of developing stomach ulcers and heart problems. Also, bulimics are more likely than anorectics to relapse; the Center for Eating Disorders in Arizona has noted the majority of their bulimic patients relapse several times in the first few years of recovery.

## Long-Run Implications

Elaine Rosenthal suffered a severe bout of anorexia in her teens, weighing only 74 pounds at the height of her illness. After forced hospitalization and treatment, Rosenthal returned [to] a normal weight and went on to resume her normal life; she graduated from nursing school, married and had children. However, starting at the age of 40, Rosenthal noticed a marked decrease in her overall health. She was constantly getting sick and was always fatigued. After visiting several doctors, Rosenthal was told her illness was due to an overall weakened system caused by her years of starvation. Rosenthal, a registered nurse, is now directing a study at her hospital of employment on how to prevent heart disease and trauma in former anorectics and bulimics.

Some eating disorder-related damage can be reversed—through vitamin supplements, prescription drugs when applicable, and exercise—but some is permanent and will never be reversed. Permanent problems include, but are not limited to: osteoporosis, excessive fatigue, increased sensitivity to prescription drugs, heart weakness, kidney damage, and incontinence.

In summary, the lifespan graph of a normal American woman should have a gradual slope, and a fairly high rate of longevity. However, a woman who suffered from an eating disorder will have a much sharper decline, and possibly an earlier death. The damage caused by severe bouts of eating disorders will stay with a woman long afterwards; problems begin to arise in the middle age, when a body begins to decrease in function normally. The added stresses of an eating disorder sharply effect the decrease in functioning, and cause a variety of problems, or amplify problems that would occur with normal aging.

*"With anorexia and bulimia, I've always been on the precipice. As long as I can keep myself from tumbling off the edge, I have nothing to fear from it."*

# Eating Disorders Are Not Necessarily Harmful

Georgie Binks

In the subsequent viewpoint, Georgie Binks, a writer in Toronto, describes her experiences with disordered eating. Off and on for more than a decade, she has starved herself or thrown up food she has eaten as a way to lose weight quickly. Binks describes the feeling she gets from disordered eating as "euphoric," and argues that what she is doing is not dangerous, but simply a bad habit.

As you read, consider the following questions:

1. What is "normal weight vomiting," as explained by the author?
2. What reasons does Binks offer for starving herself?
3. Why, according to the author, is her eating disorder not dangerous?

Reprinted from Georgie Binks, "The Joys of Anorexia," *Salon*, January 27, 2000. Reprinted with permission from *Salon*.

As far as bad habits go, if I were a pack-a-day smoker who kept falling off the wagon, I'd probably be getting friendly advice from everyone—use the patch, try hypnosis, chew this gum and if none of those worked, maybe a smoker's rights group would work.

Drink too much? Well, as long as I wasn't driving and it didn't affect my job, my friends might simply take it as an appreciation of alcohol, especially if it was good red wine that had me by the collar.

But my bad habit is one that makes everybody's eyes widen when they hear it. It is not socially acceptable, and absolutely no one has a sense of humor about it. My bad habit is that I like to starve myself from time to time. The doctors say it must be a psychological problem. Perhaps I should be looking at what I am going through when I'm depriving myself of food. But I think it is just a very effective and enjoyable form of weight loss, one that I have had control over for years now.

I think if people understood how good starving themselves feels, they would understand people with eating disorders a lot better. They would also do their best to make sure no one ever got an inkling of the feeling, because once a trip has been taken down that road, it's a difficult trip back for most people. And that's probably why, according to the National Association of Anorexia Nervosa and Associated Disorders, there are 7 million women and 1 million men who suffer from eating disorders. (They report that 6 percent of all serious cases die from the disorder.) I am one of the fortunate ones, because I have always been able to stop before it became a serious problem.

I never made a conscious effort to use starving myself as a dieting tool. I was always a skinny child because I was utterly bored with food. But at 16, I discovered fast food. My first taste of a Harvey's burger was heaven. I used to lie to my parents, pushing my plate away at dinner and telling them I was off to the library, while my friends and I headed off for a cheeseburger with extra dill pickles. After a few months, we discovered a little crepe house downtown and began to frequent it without our parents' knowledge. I gained a bit of weight, but at 5-foot-7 and 107 pounds, I definitely had nothing to worry about. I had grown quickly and my weight hadn't yet caught up with me.

## The First Flirtation with Starving

My first real flirtation with starving came during my second year at college. I admit that part of my problem was that I was in an up-and-down love affair. But it wasn't my first, so why would I start starving myself now and not for the other romances? At the beginning I simply didn't feel like eating. So for the first couple of days I just downed a Coke for breakfast and smoked a cigarette, the same for lunch and about a half a portion of dinner. After about three days I dubbed it the "Coke and cigarettes diet." After a month and a half I weighed 102, down from the 118 I had weighed when I arrived at the university. Cheekbones had replaced the baby fat on my face and my hipbones actually stood out. To this day, that is a memory I cherish.

However, my boyfriend (the up-and-down one) told me I looked awful and fortunately I believed him. Or if I didn't, I heeded his comments anyway and started eating. That summer I gained back the weight and the cheeks during my job as a waitress at a Rocky Mountains resort.

It was not until about 10 years later that starving myself came in handy again. This time there was more going on in my life than usual, but I don't think that was the issue. It started out with stomach jitters over a failed romance and a move to a new city. Not eating properly for a few days gave me that great "high" I remembered from the Coke and cigarettes days. That was what had hooked me then and what was doing it now. Doctors who work with anorexics say it's not unusual. People in concentration camps who are starving feel euphoric, but apparently it's a transient feeling that goes away after a while.

## "Normal Weight Vomiting"

During this little foray into starvation land, I lived mainly on apple juice and cigarettes. I'd mellowed in my choice of beverages, but the cigarettes were still an integral part of the diet because they were so successful at killing my appetite. This time I also started an exercise program, which helped put me down two dress sizes. In addition to that, I started what I thought was bulimia, but is known as "normal weight vomiting." (It's only called bulimia if it includes bingeing followed by throwing up.) I simply ate a normal dinner and then threw it up. The only problem with this was that while it was something I initially did on my own, it eventually turned into something my body was doing whether or not I liked it. It got to the point where I would simply eat dinner and then about 15 minutes later, I would feel ill and throw up.

## The "Benefits" of Anorexia

When one suffers from a psychological disorder, overcoming it means understanding its positive points—what you get out of having it. The most common "benefits" achieved by sufferers of anorexia nervosa as related to me over the past twenty-five years are:

- It makes me special.
- It proves I have more willpower to resist food than other girls.
- It's the only way I can say no to people (by refusing to gain weight).
- It's my assertiveness.
- I'm invisible without it.
- It's my friend.
- It gives me a sense of protection.

Steven Levenkron, *Treating and Overcoming Anorexia Nervosa*, 1997.

I went from 134 pounds to 117. Physically, I felt great. But it had its downside. One night I was asked over to an attractive man's house for dinner. He served lobster and a beautiful creamy dessert washed down with lots of wine. It was obvious he had plans for me after dinner, but by then I was throwing up so regularly that my body automatically went into action. I started to feel nauseated and I knew I had to get out of there. Fast. I arrived home just in time.

By now I was calling my little throwing up habit the "taste it twice diet." My friends did not think it was funny. One pal who joined me on a business trip and saw my after-dinner regurgitations was very upset. "You'll ruin your teeth and you could choke, you know." I curtailed my vomiting for the rest of the trip.

While my friends found it both disturbing and puzzling, I actually was happy with my successful dieting tools. They were effective and the euphoria I experienced while starving was addictive. But it all came to an end abruptly when I met my husband. It wasn't that he made me so happy that I quit. It was just that when I told him what I was doing, he became very upset and pleaded with me to stop. I did, but I was under constant surveillance. For years, if I ever got stomach flu or ate something that made me sick, he was right in there as I was throwing up, lecturing me about eating disorders.

When he moved out a couple of years ago, I wondered if I would go on my favorite diet again. I didn't. In fact, it wasn't until this spring, when I started dating a man 10 years my junior, that the starvation diet started up. Initially I was just trying to lose weight fast. The relationship was progressing at a greater speed than I had anticipated. So I was down to eating practically nothing and swimming a half mile every day.

All of a sudden, that wonderful euphoric feeling was back again. I felt terrific. I looked terrific. For three months I ate just enough to keep from fainting. Then I ended the relationship because it was becoming just a bit too much. I started eating again, but with restraint. And that's where I am now.

## An Erotic Feeling

But I'll starve myself again, for the sense of power over my body. It's almost an erotic feeling. I must admit that this summer, as I starved myself and fell in love again, I started to feel like Charlotte Rampling (feel, not look) as she wasted away in that isolated room with Dirk Bogarde in "The Night Porter." Feeling better about your body is extremely sensuous.

As I look back and read this, I notice that men seem to be involved in each one of these dieting episodes, although not in similar roles. Sometimes they are troubling, like that one during college. Sometimes they are absent and sometimes they are an exciting new beginning, as with the third. Not really any pattern.

But another thing I notice is that every bout has started off in the spring. Could the knowledge that a long Canadian winter is coming to an end be a catalyst for me to try to experience a rebirth as a new, thinner entity? Or is it just that as the parka comes off, my white, bumpy flesh is exposed to the world once again?

I think it's actually just circumstance. If I'm pushed into not eating for a day or two because of a nervous stomach, all of a sudden I find myself enjoying it. And so far, I've been able to control it, rather than have it control me.

If I'm this positive about it, would I want, say, my daughter to start starving herself? Definitely not. In fact, when she started to complain about her weight (which was perfect) a year ago, I told her all women feel fat—even the skinniest—so she shouldn't worry about it. And she stopped worrying. I don't want her to start because I'm concerned if she ever finds out how good it feels, she won't be able to quit. It is that kind of thing. If you can control it, it is a great dieting tool, but once it controls you, you're in real trouble.

I have friends who have starved themselves down to 80 pounds. I have known people who died because of their starving habit. So why do I play with it? I don't experiment with drugs that can kill me, so why do I dabble in such a dangerous dieting game? With anorexia and bulimia, I've always been on the precipice. As long as I can keep myself from tumbling off the edge, I have nothing to fear from it. And so far, I've been able to. So what's wrong with that?

# Periodical Bibliography

The following articles have been selected to supplement the diverse views presented in this chapter. Addresses are provided for periodicals not indexed in the *Readers' Guide to Periodical Literature*, the *Alternative Press Index*, the *Social Sciences Index*, or the *Index to Legal Periodicals and Books*.

| | |
|---|---|
| Bonnie Bruce and Denise Wilfley | "Binge Eating Among the Overweight Population: A Serious and Prevalent Problem," *Journal of the American Dietetic Association*, January 1996. |
| Beth Fontenot | "Consuming Disorders," *Priorities for Health*, vol. 11, no. 3, 1999. Available from 1995 Broadway, 2nd Floor, New York, NY 10023-5860. |
| David M. Garner and Anne Kearney-Cooke | "Body Image 1996: There May Be a Shift in How People View Themselves," *Psychology Today*, March 13, 1996. |
| Richard Grenier | "From Witchcraft to Modern Hysteria," *Washington Times*, May 13, 1997. |
| Beatrice Trum Hunter | "Eating Disorders: Perilous Compulsions," *Consumers' Research Magazine*, September 1997. |
| *Issues and Controversies On File* | "Eating Disorders," April 14, 2000. |
| Tracy Nesdoly | "The First Bite: Kids' Eating Disorders Are a Serious Concern," *Maclean's*, June 17, 1996. |

# CHAPTER 2

# Who Is at Risk of Eating Disorders?

# Chapter Preface

On June 30, 1997, Heidi Guenther, a twenty-two-year-old dancer for the Boston Ballet, collapsed and died—the suspected result of the effects of anorexia. According to media reports, Guenther had lost weight at the request of the ballet company's artistic director; however, she eventually became so thin that the director asked her to regain several pounds.

Although doctors were unable to confirm that Guenther died as a direct result of anorexia, the tragedy highlighted the problem of anorexia among ballet dancers. Critics maintain that the ballet culture, by prizing thinness to the point of obsession, places dancers at severe risk of developing eating disorders. Dr. Linda Hamilton, a clinical psychologist who publishes a regular column in *Dance Magazine*, approximates that 4 to 15 percent of dancers experience eating disorders, compared to 1 to 3 percent of the general population.

Other activities that revere thinness, such as gymnastics, ice skating, and running, face similar criticisms. Eating disorder experts often condemn these sports for fostering the belief that a thinner physique leads to improved athletic performance—a belief that leads some athletes to severely curtail their food intake while maintaining rigorous exercise routines. Such practices can cause the "female athlete triad": loss of menstruation, osteoporosis, and disordered eating.

On the other hand, some studies suggest that participation in sports can prevent eating disorders. Women who are active in sports, a recent survey by the Commonwealth Fund asserts, are less likely to develop eating disorders than are women who diet instead of exercising. Benita Fitzgerald Mosely, president of the Women's Sports Foundation and a three-time Olympian, argues that "sports can actually act as a deterrent to eating disorders, because girls who participate in athletics benefit from higher than average levels of self-esteem. Women who were active in sports and recreational activities as girls generally have increased confidence and self-esteem and a more positive body image."

In the following chapter, authors examine in greater depth the connection between athletics and eating disorders. The chapter also discusses several other risk factors for the development of these disorders.

*"Between one-third and one-half of . . .
teenage women whose weight was normal
perceived themselves as overweight."*

# Adolescent Girls Are at Risk of Eating Disorders

Suzanne Abraham and Derek Llewellyn-Jones

In the following viewpoint, Suzanne Abraham and Derek Llewellyn-Jones explain why eating disorders are prevalent among adolescent girls. During adolescence, girls typically gain weight. Meanwhile, they are highly susceptible to cultural messages emphasizing thinness as a desirable physical characteristic. In their attempt to achieve an ideal body image, the authors write, many teenage girls turn to dangerous methods of weight control, which puts them at risk of developing an eating disorder. Abraham and Llewellyn-Jones, both of whom work in the department of obstetrics and gynecology at the University of Sydney, are authors of the book *Eating Disorders: The Facts*, from which this viewpoint is excerpted.

As you read, consider the following questions:

1. According to the authors, what is "the adolescent girl's dilemma"?
2. How do adolescents misperceive their body shape and size, as stated by Abraham and Llewellyn-Jones?
3. As cited by the authors, what are the methods by which teenage girls control their weight?

For most of recorded history a woman was seen as desirable when her body was plump due to the deposition of fat on her breasts, hips, thighs, and abdomen. It was fashionable to be fat. The cultural belief that to be fat was to be attractive was due to the uncertainty of food supplies in pre-industrial and early industrial societies, to the irregular occurrence of famines, and to the effects of diseases which eliminated large numbers of farm labourers. A curvaceous female body indicated that the husband (or father) was prudent, efficient, and affluent. It also indicated that the woman was prepared for times of food shortage. Her family would be protected because she had sufficient food stored in her storeroom to meet the shortage, and she herself had sufficient energy, stored in her body in the form of fat, to look after her family.

In the past 75 years, with abundant food supplies and good food distribution in most of the developed nations of the Western world, almost for the first time in history slimness has begun to become fashionable. This is documented in fashion magazines and in records of the 'vital statistics' of women winning beauty contests. For the past three decades the public perception has been that a woman is attractive, desirable, and successful when she is slim. A study of the vital statistics of *Playboy* centre-folds and of competitors in the finals and the winners of the Miss America Pageant Contest over the past 25 years shows that, although the preferred breast size has varied, and there has been a slight increase in the height of the women, their weights have decreased and are below the average of American women of similar age and height.

Over the same period, articles on 'new and exciting' diets (often nutritionally inadequate and occasionally dangerous) have appeared at regular intervals in women's magazines, and the number is increasing. The publication of 'new and revolutionary' diet books is also increasing.

## The Media and Perception of Body Shape

Most people living in the developed nations also receive a constant stream of impressions from television commercials which use young, attractive, and lissom women to advertise products as diverse as soft drinks, security investments, cars, cigarettes, computers, fast foods, floor polishers etc.

The messages from the media stress how desirable it is for women to be young and to be or to become thin. These messages particularly influence teenage women at a period when they are undergoing emotional stress as they seek to achieve independence from their parents, to compete with their peers, and to find their identity. Adolescence is a time of concern about body image. Achieving the ideal body image is thought to ensure success and happiness.

## Hormonal Changes in Adolescence

In late childhood hormonal changes trigger an increase in height in girls and boys. The increase, or growth spurt, occurs at an earlier age in girls than boys and is achieved by the child increasing the amount of food he or she eats. In girls the onset of the growth spurt precedes the onset of menstruation and overlaps its establishment at an average age of 12½ years. There is a wide time range in the onset and duration of the growth spurt and the peak may be reached by girls as early as age 10 or as late as age 15 years. The growth spurt is accompanied by marked changes in the bodily appearance of the two sexes, which in turn are dependent on the sex hormones which are now being produced in the girl's ovaries or the boy's testicles. Both sexes show an increase in muscle bulk but this is much more marked in boys. Girls have a particularly large spurt in hip growth and, in contrast to boys, do not lose fat during the growth spurt. In fact, girls have a general tendency to increase their body fat, particularly on the upper legs, as they cease to gain height. Fat is also deposited beneath the skin, in the breasts and over the hips. Obviously the amount of fat deposited is related to the energy absorbed from the food the girl eats and is influenced by the hormonal changes which are occurring at this time. Energy intake from food is limited by the person's appetite. During early adolescence, unknown factors stimulate the teenager to eat more, with the consequence that the energy intake for girls reaches a maximum during the age range of 11 to 14, at a time when her energy needs are great. From about the age of 14, a teenage girl's energy needs fall, but if she continues to eat the same amount as she has been eating she will absorb an excess of energy which will be converted into fat, and she will become fat. She has to control her food intake, in order to control her weight.

This is the adolescent girl's dilemma. She may wish to remain thin or to become thin, because cultural norms expect her to be thin, or she may reject those norms, either because of conflict within herself or within her family, or because she enjoys and finds emotional release in eating. If she chooses to become and remain thin, she has to learn new eating habits, because she will inevitably become fat if she continues eating the quantity of food she has become used to eating.

## Adolescents' Perception of Body Shape and Size

A young woman's perception of her body is important to her psychological well-being. She may see her body as large and overweight compared with those of fashionable and popular media personalities. It is significant that, in contrast to older women, adolescent girls perceive their bodies part by part, noting particularly the size and shape of their breasts and the size of their thighs, bottom, hips, and abdomen. The thighs are particularly vulnerable to an overperception of size—the girl perceiving her thighs as larger and uglier than they usually are.

The overperception of body size is found amongst teenage girls in many countries. In a Swedish study of the entire female population of a small town, in the late 1960s, 26 per cent of 14-year-olds perceived themselves as fat; and among the 18-year-olds, over 50 per cent reported that they were fat. In the USA in the 1970s a study of 1000 teenagers attending high school showed that the girls were particularly preoccupied with their body shape and their weight. About half of them classified themselves as obese, although anthropometric measurements showed that only 25 per cent were obese by the criteria used by the authors, which were based on standard US weight, height, and age tables.

In the mid-1980s, in the USA, 2500 teenage women aged 15 to 18 were surveyed. There had been little change in perceptions about body shape and weight and attitudes to being fat. Forty-three per cent of the girls perceived themselves as overweight and 31 per cent feared that they looked fat. Eighty-two per cent wanted to lose weight, 39 per cent worried about overeating and 18 per cent were fearful they would gain weight.

Another US study made in 1991 confirmed this finding. In this study, 60 per cent of the school students (mean age 16) described themselves as being overweight; 75 per cent wanted to lose weight; 80 per cent said that they were above the weight at which they would be happiest.

Two Australian studies conducted in the early 1990s of over 900 adolescent women reported similar findings. The investigations showed that between one-third and one-half of the teenage women whose weight was normal perceived themselves as overweight.

It is apparent from these studies that the attitudes of young women in these three developed countries about their body shape and weight have not changed in the past two decades.

Faced with this preoccupation about their body shape and weight, it appears that between one-third and two-thirds of all teenage women in the USA and similar developed countries, go on diets and one woman in six diets 'seriously'.

## Adolescent and Young People's Eating Behaviour

We have been interested in teenage and young people's eating behaviour for the past 15 years. A study made in Sydney in 1981 showed that Australian women students aged 18 to 22 decreased their intake of carbohydrate, protein, and fat, and hence of energy, in the early premenstrual period but increased their intake in the day or two before and during menstruation. Individual women showed a wide daily variation in food intake, the amount eaten depending on how the women felt. Many women have feelings of well-being in the week after menstruation and decrease their food intake during this time. Later in the menstrual cycle, that is in the two weeks after ovulation has occurred, they feel hungry and eat more food, or even start binge-eating.

The Sydney study showed that the daily quantity of food eaten could vary fourfold. In the Swedish study quoted earlier, one-third of the teenage girls alternated dieting with periods of binge eating; and such eating behaviour was more common among the older teenage girls.

We also asked four groups of Australian young women aged 15 to 25 to complete a questionnaire about their eating habits, menstrual status, and the behaviour which they used to control their weight. The groups were students, ballet dancers, anorexia nervosa patients, and bulimia nervosa patients. Of the 106 students surveyed, 94 per cent had tried to diet at some time, the majority first trying between the ages of 13 and 18. Seventy-nine per cent said that they wanted to be a little or a lot lighter in weight and 31 per cent said that they had difficulty in controlling their weight.

In 1988 another study of Australian women aged 19 to 29 showed that over 50 per cent had experienced difficulty in controlling their weight at some time. Four out of every ten teenagers considered that they had an on-going problem of weight control and one in three felt that the problem interfered with their daily lives. Like the Swedish and the American teenagers and young women, most of the Australian women wanted to lose weight from their thighs, bottom, hips, and abdomen. Sixty-three per cent of the Australian young women said that they had episodes of overeating when they 'couldn't stop'. Eighteen per cent of the teenagers aged 15 to 18, and 23 per cent of the women aged 18 to 26 were habitual 'binge-eaters'. One woman in ten, aged 18 to 26 considered that binge-eating was a great problem for them. To control their weight most of the Australian young women avoided eating between meals, took energetic exercise, kept busy to avoid the temptation to eat, missed out one (or more) meals each day, chose low-calorie foods, or [used] other methods.

Many of the 900 young women (mean age 15) surveyed in the two Australian studies had disturbed eating behaviour. One third had been on 'crash diets' or had episodes of fasting, and half 'avoided meals'. Twenty three per cent of the women had used 'pathological weight control behaviours' and 10 per cent smoked 'to lose weight'.

The weight control measures described are similar to those used by women who have an eating disorder such as the binge-eating disorder, bulimia nervosa, or anorexia nervosa.

Disturbed eating behaviour affects young as well as older teenagers. In 1994 the eating behaviours of 200 Australian boys and 300 girls aged 10–14 years old were surveyed. The girls were divided into two groups: those who were prepubertal, that is they had not started menstruating, and those who had passed their menarche. The results showed that 16 per cent of the prepubertal girls and 40 per cent of the girls who had passed their menarche perceived themselves as too fat. Nineteen per cent of the boys also perceived themselves as too fat. In an attempt to control their weight most of those surveyed had used sensible methods of weight control, but 20 per cent of the girls and 9 per cent of the boys used extreme methods, including smoking.

It is evident from these studies that in several Western countries, most young women (and some young men) are unnecessarily concerned about their body shape and believe they have a problem with their weight. These concerns lead them to take measures to lose weight, even though their actual weight is in the normal range. It also appears that anxieties about body shape and weight are being expressed at an earlier age than a decade ago.

## How Adolescents Control Their Body Shape and Weight

Although concern about body shape and weight is occurring among younger teenagers, on average, teenage women first become aware of their body shape and weight at the age of 14.6 years. About a year later, many young women start trying simple and safe methods of weight control, such as not snacking between meals and exercising. By the age of 16.4 years young women may start on a diet which they believe will be successful in enabling them to lose weight.

Most women diet for shorter or longer periods, with about a quarter of those who diet doing so 'seriously'. Some women (14–30 per cent) fast for periods of time, usually a day or two, to try to reduce their weight quickly. Some women (25–65 per cent) exercise to lose weight and to change their body shape. About three women in every hundred self-induce vomiting, and between 1 and 5 per cent abuse laxatives.

By the age of 17 the minority of adolescent women who

are having serious problems with eating, body shape, and body weight, recognize the fact. These women try the various methods of weight control just mentioned but the frequent use of dangerous methods of weight control, such as self-induced vomiting and laxative abuse, do not start until the young woman is aged 18.6 on average, and if chosen most young women will have used one or more of them by the age of 22.

As well as restricting food intake and exercising to lose weight, a number of women (variously reported as 14 to 46 per cent) go on eating binges, usually starting at about the age of 18. . . .

## The Onset of Eating Disorders

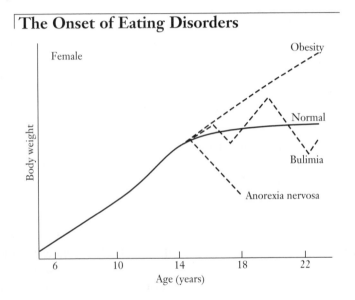

Suzanne Abraham and Derek Llewellyn-Jones, *Eating Disorders: The Facts*, 1997.

Some young women intersperse periods of strict dieting by episodes of gross overeating, or binge-eating, probably because their body responds to the lack of food by altering its physiology. The changes in diet send messages to a centre in the brain which increases the physiological pressure to eat, and often to overeat or binge. In most cases the eating binges are infrequent and do not affect the young woman's quality of life or her life-style. In some cases her quality of life is affected and she loses control over her eating behaviour, which may result in the development of the binge-eating disorder or of bulimia nervosa, which may disrupt the life of the woman considerably and, if dangerous methods of weight control—self-induced vomiting and laxative or diuretic abuse—are used, may lead to serious illness.

Other young women are so concerned about losing control of their eating behaviour that they starve themselves and start on a relentless pursuit of thinness. They eat minimal amounts of food, and many use the dangerous methods of weight control mentioned earlier. The result is that they become emaciated and their menstrual periods cease. They develop anorexia nervosa.

Although these two disorders predominantly affect young women in Western countries, recent research shows that the same problems are becoming increasingly diagnosed among all social classes and ethnic groups. For example, the eating disorders are being diagnosed amongst young women in Japan and some other Asian countries.

Those teenagers who choose to ignore the social pressures to become and to remain thin, and continue eating more energy than they need for their bodily functions, gain weight progressively and become obese. In fact a person who is grossly obese has at least 1260 MJ (300 000kcals) of energy stored in her body as fat. . . .

The disordered eating behaviour usually starts between the ages of 14 and 18. We would stress that the binge-eating disorder, anorexia nervosa, bulimia nervosa, and obesity (especially morbid obesity)—are not *illnesses* in themselves. They become illnesses when they interfere with the person's physical or mental comfort; of if they are likely to produce severe medical complications; or disorganize the person's life to a marked degree; or so distort her or his life that close relatives are also involved and help is sought. Unfortunately, in severe cases, unless treatment is sought the eating disorder may lead to a premature death of the victim.

*"It's not unusual for kids in elementary and middle school to become anorexic or bulimic."*

# Preteens Are at Risk of Eating Disorders

Daryn Eller

Daryn Eller, a freelance writer who lives in Santa Barbara, California, maintains in the following viewpoint that preteens as young as elementary school-age are increasingly developing eating disorders. Studies show that many pre-adolescent children exhibit dissatisfaction with their bodies and have attempted to diet, writes Eller.

As you read, consider the following questions:
1. What are the classic symptoms of a full-blown eating disorder, as stated by the author?
2. In one study cited by Eller, how many first-, third-, and fifth-graders had been on a diet?
3. Which girls feel most self-conscious about their bodies, according to Eller?

Reprinted from Daryn Eller, "Detecting Eating Disorders," *Parents*, August 1998. Reprinted with permission from the author.

There have been enough TV movies, magazine articles, and unfortunate high-profile deaths to put eating disorders on most parents' radar screens. But if you're the parent of a preteen, they may appear as distant blips. After all, anorexia (a drastic reduction in food intake resulting in extreme weight loss) and bulimia (purging by vomiting, using laxatives or diuretics, or by excessive exercise) are teenage problems, right?

Wrong. "We used to see eating disorders mostly in young college-age women," says Barbara Fleming, coordinator for the National Eating Disorders Organization, in Tulsa. "Now it's not unusual for kids in elementary and middle school to become anorexic or bulimic." The National Institute of Mental Health estimates that 1 percent of adolescent girls suffer from anorexia and that an additional 2 to 3 percent are bulimic. (Girls are the primary victims of this disease, although the incidence among boys is on the rise.)

Your preteen may not exhibit the classic symptoms of a full-blown eating disorder—obsessively counting fat grams and calories; frequently chewing gum or sucking on candy (to quell hunger); wearing baggy, body-disguising clothes; always making excuses to go to the bathroom after meals; saying derogatory things about her body; or ceasing to menstruate. But that doesn't mean you don't have to worry. "Most parents will not be faced with the enormous challenges of dealing with an anorexic or bulimic," says Julia A. Graber, Ph.D., associate director of the Adolescent Study Program at Columbia University, in New York City. "Many, however, will face the challenges of children who have poor body images or eating problems like excessive dieting, which are associated with lesser, but still unhealthy, outcomes."

## Problems with Body Image Can Start in Grade School

Puberty is a catalyst for body-image and eating disorders, but studies show that many kids already have weight concerns by the time they enter this turbulent stage. In 1996, researchers at Connecticut College, in New London, asked first-, third-, and fifth-graders questions about their bodies and related behavior. Forty percent of the first-graders, 50 percent of the third-graders, and 66 percent of the fifth-graders said they'd been on a diet. When asked whether they agreed or disagreed with the statement "I like what I look like in pictures," 91 percent of the first-graders agreed, but only 77 percent of the third-graders and 52 percent of the fifth-graders did. "When kids get to the age where they think about what members of the opposite sex think of them, their self-esteem starts to go down," says lead researcher Joan Chrisler, Ph.D.

---

### Young Girls with Diabetes at Eating Disorder Risk

Adolescent girls with diabetes are more than twice as likely to have an eating disorder as other girls their same age, researchers report.

While about 4% of non-diabetic adolescent girls in a new study had an eating disorder, 10% of girls with type 1 diabetes had such a problem, according to findings published in the June 10th, 2000, issue of the *British Medical Journal.* . . .

Diabetic girls are also twice as likely to have "subthreshold" eating disorders—abnormal eating patterns that did not meet the full criteria for a diagnosable disorder. While 14% of diabetic girls had subthreshold eating disorders, only 8% of non-diabetic girls had similar conditions.

Yahoo! News, June 9, 2000. Available at http://dailynews.yahoo.com/h/nm/20000609/hl/diabetes_children_1.html.

---

Couple these early perceptions with the physical disruption of puberty and it's not surprising that body loathing peaks during ages 11 through 13—particularly in girls, who experience not only the growth of breasts and pubic hair and the onset of menstruation but also the normal weight gain that accompanies these changes.

### Early Puberty Raises the Risk

Among the girls who often feel most self-conscious are those who mature early, a factor that puts them at particular risk for eating disorders. In a study published in 1997, researchers at Columbia University found that 3.5 percent of the girls who developed early had eating disorders, while only .8 percent of normal or late developers did. "Early maturers tend to be more concerned with what boys find attractive than on-time girls, so they may begin to control their weight as a means of being more appealing," says Dr. Graber. Extreme weight loss can also be a way for girls to desexualize their bodies and avoid sexual pressures or feelings.

Pressures of all types—sexual, social, academic—mount in the preteen years. "A lot of kids can cope, but some, especially girls who aren't feeling too competent in other areas, can get more and more distressed about how they look," says Michelle Friedman, who leads the eating-disorders team at North Shore Children's Hospital, in Salem, Massachusetts. Many anorexics control their weight because they feel so powerless to control other aspects of their lives. And yet emotional ups and downs are typical at this age. So how can parents tell when their preteen has crossed from normal insecurity into dangerous self-hatred?

"Just about all teenagers say they look or feel fat," says Friedman, "but if there's an intense preoccupation with food, weight, and exercise, and you see it affecting many different facets of your child's life, that's a problem."

Have a talk with your child to gauge what's going on, suggests Linda Jones-Hicks, M.D., director of adolescent medicine at the University of Medicine and Dentistry of New Jersey, in Stratford. Ask specific questions about her behavior, such as "Aren't you hungry? You left half your food on your plate" or "How many hours a day are you exercising?" If she is unusually angry or defensive, take it as a warning and consider a professional evaluation.

*"Anorexia is now known to affect women in their 30s, 40s, and 50s."*

# Adult Women Are at Risk of Eating Disorders

Leslie Vreeland

In the subsequent viewpoint, Leslie Vreeland argues that the majority of eating disorder sufferers are adult women over the age of thirty—some of whom developed the problem during adolescence and others who acquired it in adulthood. According to the author, age-related weight gain, which leads some women to diet and exercise compulsively, often triggers the disorder. Vreeland is a journalist and adjunct faculty member of New York University's department of journalism.

As you read, consider the following questions:
1. How common are eating disorders, as claimed by the author?
2. According to Vreeland, why is adult anorexia so often misdiagnosed or not noticed?
3. As stated by the author, how do relatives of an eating-disordered woman unintentionally perpetuate the disease?

Excerpted from Leslie Vreeland, "Dying to Be Thin—After 30," *Good Housekeeping*, March 1, 1998. Reprinted with permission from the author.

Sheri Glazier, a 31-year-old nursery-school teacher and mother of three in Bangor, ME, had always watched what she ate. At 100 pounds and five feet tall, she was never especially thin. But slowly, her attitude toward food began to grow bizarre. She started skipping meals and stocking the cellar with exotic cookies and imported pasta—a kind of shrine to food that she never ate. Cooking became her passion, yet she always had an excuse for not eating. Over the next seven years, her weight dropped to a mere 47 pounds. Though she continually denied that she needed help, she was hospitalized nearly 25 times for dehydration and malnutrition. The condition took a toll not only on her body, but also on her family. Because she was often too weak to care for her children, they began pulling away from her, relying on their father instead.

## Adult Anorexia

This is anorexia nervosa in an adult. It's an insidious eating disorder, in which victims are so afraid of gaining weight that they starve themselves, sometimes to death (about 10 to 15 percent die from complications). Though it's usually associated with teenagers, anorexia is now known to affect women in their 30s, 40s, and 50s. In fact, some experts say that while anorexia typically begins in adolescence, the majority of sufferers are adults, because the condition tends to be chronic. But it can also strike for the first time in adulthood. The trigger is often age-related weight gain, which leads some women to diet strenuously—the provocateur to developing an eating disorder.

Even more alarming, new research suggests that anorexia—a disorder that affects women disproportionately—is twice as common as doctors once thought. Half a million women have it, and many more have several symptoms, such as a compulsive need to exercise several hours every day. Despite its prevalence, adult anorexia is sometimes misdiagnosed—or missed entirely.

"Anorexics are not always startlingly underweight," says B. Timothy Walsh, M.D., a professor of psychiatry at Columbia University and director of the Eating Disorder Research Unit of the New York State Psychiatric Institute.

In a society that prizes thinness, anorexics are often just slim enough to look good in clothes, and they often get away with blaming their weight loss on stress. When women with the disorder begin losing weight, they train themselves to tune out their hunger by exercising vigorously and congratulating themselves for the accomplishment of resisting food, says psychiatrist Catherine Halmi, M.D., director of the eating disorders unit at New York Hospital-Cornell Medical Center in White Plains, NY. Once anorexics become emaciated and weak, they lose their appetites entirely, making weight gain difficult.

## Genetics, Personality, and Biology

How do they manage to diet hyper-successfully while millions struggle with being overweight? Scientists suspect that genetics, personality, and biology may play important roles. Sisters of anorexics are at a more than three times greater risk for developing the disorder, and identical twins are more susceptible than fraternal twins, who are genetically different. Also prone to anorexia are perfectionists, as well as people who are overly controlling or unable to express emotions. Some research suggests that a disturbance in brain chemistry may be responsible. The evidence: Anorexics respond well to antidepressants that help stabilize the brain chemical serotonin, which regulates mood and appetite.

As promising as these new findings may be, they won't count for much if anorexics refuse treatment. Patients work hard at covering their tracks, because controlling their weight becomes the foundation of their self-esteem. Often families and friends aren't aware there is a problem—or at least nothing that the anorexic can't somehow "cure" herself. Other times, family members and friends do realize something is amiss, but their attempts to help are angrily rebuffed, says Mary Hopper, M.A., a therapist at The Renfrew Center in Philadelphia. In the face of so much pain and frustration, relatives often deny the illness along with the patient, unintentionally perpetuating it.

"A husband will notice his wife is losing weight," says Hopper. "He may even say, 'You look great.' As she grows thinner, he might say, 'My God, you're flesh and bones.' But he doesn't realize that's just a challenge for her to diet more."

Gradually, the husband may stop mentioning his wife's weight. "He may be afraid that if he confronts his wife, she'll restrict food even more," she explains.

## Midlife Triggers

Although a small number of women with eating disorders develop them for the first time in midlife, most have a history of such problems dating back to their teens or twenties. Whether symptoms are a relapse or the first onset of an eating disorder, experts agree that midlife stresses can be a trigger.

Like puberty, menopause changes a woman's image of herself as a sexual being. "At 13 the question is, what does it mean to have a period?" explains David Herzog, M.D., director of the Eating Disorder Unit at Massachusetts General Hospital and associate professor of psychiatry at Harvard Medical School. "And at menopause, what does it mean *not* to?"

Adolescents sometimes stop eating in the hope that they won't develop a womanly shape, which they perceive as ugly and fat. In fact, many girls with anorexia *do* stop developing breasts and menstruating. Mature women with eating disorders may be expressing similar anxieties that they've managed to suppress for years. They, too, may express conflicts about sex by either overeating or undereating.

Another contributor to eating disorders in midlife is the social pressure to stay young. There is a natural tendency for both men and women to gain weight as they age—in part because metabolism slows. But in our society, weight gain and aging in women are considered taboo. This makes it more difficult to accept the aging process. "What used to be considered an acceptable shape is no longer acceptable," says Dr. Herzog. "And some women are single at midlife, which can make them more self-conscious about their looks."

Joel M. Roselin, *Seasons*, vol. 7, no. 5.

Indeed, confronting an anorexic in denial can be risky, so family members often don't. Diane Litynski, 36, of Poughkeepsie, NY, has been battling the disorder for a decade. She says her family never even mentioned her weight. Her husband used trainer talk: "He would coach me in my running," says the former distance runner. "The most he ever said was, 'Your upper body needs to be built up about fifteen pounds.'"

Friends also don't know what to say that can make a difference. Caroline Polsenberg, 33, of Haddon Township, NJ, who has struggled with the disorder since her teens, reports that when drastic weight loss occurred, "Friends would ask, 'Are you okay?' and I'd say I was fine." Others mistakenly assume that they can't help.

## The Need for Appropriate Treatment

More than anything, an anorexic needs prompt appropriate treatment. With counseling and medication, about one third are cured. Another third improve but never fully recover, and the rest wage a lifelong battle. The longer an anorexic takes to get help, the harder healing will be. "The disorder starts with weight loss, but it expands to affect a person's relationships and her performance on the job," explains Dr. Walsh. "In the end, the victim has to restructure her entire life—not just her relationship with food."

For women in the early stages, professional counseling may suffice. Women with full-blown anorexia need cognitive behavioral therapy, which teaches them to change their actions and attitudes toward food. Sometimes they require antidepressants. Also recommended are nutritional counseling, family therapy, and regular doctor visits to monitor progress. Such treatment can cost between $5,000 and $10,000 per year. Although some insurers are willing to pay for antidepressants, many are reluctant to cover other treatments.

Long-term hospitalization is necessary when weight loss is life-threatening. Unfortunately, few patients receive this standard of care because many insurers are reluctant to pick up the $1,000-per-day tab that effective treatment tends to cost. "Few insurers pay for anything more than 'medical stabilization'—the week to ten days it takes to replace fluids lost to dehydration," says Stewart Agras, M.D., professor of psychiatry at Stanford University and director of its eating disorders unit. "But it takes six to twelve weeks for patients to regain significant weight.". . .

Ultimately, the cure may lie within the patient. For Sheri Glazier, now 50, her last hospitalization was the turning point. "One night, I dreamed that if the anorexia continued, I would die. I thought about my children, and I realized that

I wanted to be there for them." That insight prompted her to seek treatment for 60 days at an eating-disorders clinic in Florida. There, she finally began to fight her illness—and eventually won. "There was nothing magical about the place," she stresses. "It's just that I was finally ready to accept what they had to offer."

*"Eating disorders are more common among female athletes than in the general population, as high as 60 percent in sports in which low body weight or ideal body shape confer, or are perceived to confer, an advantage."*

# Female Athletes Are at Risk of Eating Disorders

Renée Despres

According to Renée Despres, the author of the following viewpoint, statistics reveal that eating disorders are a serious problem among female athletes. In fact, claims Despres, most competitive female runners suffer from some type of disordered eating. She states that sports in which slimness is perceived as an advantage—including gymnastics, figure skating, ballet, bodybuilding, rock climbing, and distance running—foster eating disorders. Over-exercise combined with low caloric intake can impair athletes' performance and mental acuity and cause long-term health problems. Despres is a contributing editor for *Women's Sports & Fitness*, a monthly magazine for women who participate in sports.

As you read, consider the following questions:
1. What is "activity anorexia," as defined by the author?
2. What does Despres cite as the warning signs of an eating disorder in female athletes?
3. According to Despres, how do eating disorders compromise an athlete's performance and health?

Excerpted from Renée Despres, "Burn Baby Burn," *Women's Sports & Fitness*, May 1997. Reprinted with permission from the author.

For this particular woman, it all began in high school. She would arise before dawn and slip into her running clothes. Sliding from a slow jog to a full run, she felt the pavement beneath her feet, the strength in her legs as she climbed the first hill. She welcomed the chance to burn the calories—400 of them, if she had measured and calculated everything right—in last night's salad. To make sure every last calorie had been burned, she ran for an hour and a half.

At home, she stripped in front of the bathroom mirror, forcing herself to look at the belly that still protruded in front of jutting hipbones. At least she could count every rib. Her thighs jiggled as she slapped them lightly. She slapped harder. Fat, fat, fat. I hate my thighs, she thought. She slapped until bruises appeared, black-and-blue tendrils on the white skin.

Her mother forced her to eat a bowl of puffed wheat and skim milk before leaving, so she threw her lunch in the trash on her way to school. She didn't want the temptation of food in her locker all day. A celery stick and a carrot stick were permitted after school before the next workout, and salad for dinner. Maybe tonight she would vary the salad a little. No, that sounded scary. She knew she wouldn't gain any weight as long as she ran the same route and ate the same foods every day.

Today, more women participate in sports than at any other time in history. They are running, swimming, cycling, rowing, dancing, playing ball and more. They are testing their limits and setting new records. But for some women, the point of each day's workout is not just to achieve an athletic goal, but to burn off flesh. For some, fitness has come to mean complete subjugation of body and appetite.

For competitive and recreational athletes alike, the line between fitness and famine is a blurry one. Women athletes are set up for difficulties with food in ways that most women are not, says Katherine Fulkerson, Ph.D., a clinical psychologist who specializes in eating disorders. Eating disorders are more common among female athletes than in the general population, as high as 60 percent in sports in which low body weight or ideal body shape confer, or are perceived to confer, an advantage.

But that statistic represents only the clinical cases. How many "normal" women athletes live their lives in thrall to food and exercise obsessions? "It's the chicken-or-the-egg question," Fulkerson says. "The same kind of people who are driven to exercise and be disciplined are also most at risk of developing an eating disorder."

Indeed, a dramatic new study that Fulkerson cites shows that exercise is associated with a higher risk of eating disorders, a phenomenon researchers call "activity anorexia." When researchers exercised rats past a certain point, the rats' appetites decreased while their desire for activity increased, beginning a downward spiral toward starvation. "This research seems to lend credence to the idea that exercise at a high level could put athletes at a higher risk," Fulkerson says. "But I've still got some questions because the research wasn't based on human athletes. And not all athletes become eating disordered."

## Certain Sports Environments Foster Eating Disorders

Fulkerson points out that certain sports clearly create environments that foster eating problems. She divides high-risk sports into three categories: sports in which slim body image is part of the performance, including gymnastics, figure skating and ballet; sports in which subtle kinds of eating disorders are built in, such as bodybuilding; and sports such as rock climbing and distance running, in which there is believed to be some advantage conveyed by being lighter.

Elite masters marathoner Jane Welzel first encountered the athletic culture of thinness when she began running in college. "I never thought about dieting or anything like that for the first 18 years of my life," Welzel says. "But when I began running in college, I suddenly found myself in a sports environment where I had to focus on it. We were weighed in. I had never had so many foods to pick from as in the dining hall. I didn't know what to do, and when I looked for someone to tell me what to do, I discovered that other women on other teams were maintaining weight by bingeing and purging, or eating ice cream and not eating meals."

Caught in the weight-obsessed environment of collegiate

running, Welzel found herself disappearing into anorexia. "I eliminated 99 percent of foods from my diet. It got to the point where it was just bad to eat. I wished I could just give up food," she says. "But you can't not eat. You have to deal with it every day. To this day, I can't just enjoy eating without thinking I'm going to have to pay for this, I'm going to lose control. It doesn't run my life like it used to, but the thoughts are still there. I don't believe that I will ever be normal about food."

The struggle is particularly difficult before a big race, says Welzel, who won the marathon national championship in 1990. "It's scary. I've worked really hard and trained right, but when I'm tapering, I often think I could blow it, get fat this week," she explains. "Or I've wanted to be skinny on the line and didn't eat enough during the week before and paid for it in the race. Emotionally, it's extremely difficult for me to cut back on training and pick up on eating. I have to remember that my real goal is performance, not being skinny. If I frame it in that way, I can do it."

She's not alone in her struggle. "Even at the elite level, we talk about food and body weight all the time," she says. "We appear to be healthy and normal. But when people come up to me and say, 'You're running 100 miles a week; you can probably eat whatever you want,' I look at them and think, 'If you only knew.'

"There are a few elite women runners who have what is probably a 'normal' relationship with food. But I don't know if there are any who don't worry about it to some extent," Welzel says. "The majority have a totally dysfunctional relationship with food. And when I say 'normal,' I mean relative to my own unhealthy relationship to food. I wouldn't know what a truly normal relationship with food would look like."

She ran and walked determinedly in the pre-dawn mist, dragging her injured leg. She had risen an hour earlier than usual so she could complete her customary route, despite the pain in her hip. She had begun swimming for two hours after her classes at the university were over, just in case she didn't burn enough calories on her morning walk/run. When Dr. B. suggested she stop exercising for a few weeks, she felt a tight fear in her throat: She would get fat.

She was thin, very thin, and she knew it. She didn't want to stop eating again, but she would have to if she couldn't run anymore.

She was careful about her diet. She avoided the dormitory dining hall, with its immense salad bar, oil-laden dressings, starchy entrées, high-fat peanut butter and ice cream. Instead, she ate dinner in the seclusion of her room, cooking in her hot pot, storing frozen peas and milk in her tiny refrigerator. That way, she was able to preserve her nightly food ritual: a bowl of oatmeal with skim milk, one-third cup of cooked peas and, for dessert, six gingersnaps, a pear and four Ritz crackers. She added up the calories every night. On days the pool was closed, she skipped her only other food of the day, a dry bagel and plain yogurt.

Late at night she stared at calculus problems and tried to read Homer's *Iliad*, without much success. Schoolwork just didn't seem important. Food kept creeping into her thoughts, no matter how hard she tried to push it back. Sometimes she would give in and read the recipes in a women's magazine.

## The "Tyranny of Slenderness"

It's the pervasiveness of the cultural ideal of thinness—what eating-disorder expert Kim Chernin has called the "tyranny of slenderness"—that troubles Marvel Harrison, Ph.D., R.D., national director of Life Balance, a program for those who suffer from disordered eating. "There are a few cases that are life-or-death, in which forced, tube or intravenous feeding is necessary," Harrison says. "But that's just a handful of people compared with the huge number of women who are struggling to different degrees. Women are devoting an incredible amount of energy to controlling their bodies through exercise and diet, obsessing about calories consumed and burned. When the compulsion to exercise gets in the way of relationships, work, family and other activities, that's a problem."

Harrison argues that the level of activity itself is not the problem. "It has more to do with one's attitude about exercising than the number of hours spent exercising," she says. "Clearly there are many women in competition who wouldn't be if they didn't exercise at that level. But there's a different style of risk around obsessive exercising. Usually a person is trying to fill an emptiness, if you will, that leads to food and exercise compulsions."

## Returning to a Healthy Balance

The good news is that usually, giving up activities is not the answer. "Telling someone who exercises too much to stop is like telling somebody who overeats not to eat," Harrison says. "It doesn't make sense." The answer lies in returning to a healthy balance.

But Fulkerson says finding that "healthy balance" for women athletes can be extremely confusing. "Training demands for most athletes sound just incredibly high, particularly to a therapist unfamiliar with the requirements of an athletic career," she explains. "The therapist hears that this woman is exercising two hours a day, and to him it's off the end of the spectrum. A lot of the definitions of eating disorders come from people who don't exercise at all. How do you know when a person is doing too much activity? Not eating enough food? Athletes are by their very nature pushing limits."

Standard diagnostic criteria for eating disorders rely heavily on body weight. Most clinicians classify someone who is 15 percent or more below normal body weight as eating disordered. "At the higher levels of sports such as running, gymnastics, figure skating and ballet dancing," Fulkerson observes, "the majority of athletes are very close to that percentage. But that doesn't necessarily qualify them as anorexics."

For athletes, eating disorders warrant a different definition. "When exercise and eating cease to be goal driven and the point is just to be thinner, when the focus is on how much you're eating and how much you need to exercise to get it off, then the activity has gone past being an athletic endeavor and instead becomes part of an eating disorder," Fulkerson says. "This might not include people who are very thin."

## Warning Signs

"The warning signs I look for are body image distortion, an overconcern with eating, and no menstrual periods. Having regular menstrual cycles is a critical factor, because when periods stop, problems such as osteoporosis are likely to develop.

If you know that you're not having periods—and that this will cause problems later—then the desire to exercise becomes a pathological drive to which long-term health is sacrificed."

Fulkerson, a middle-distance runner herself, runs regularly with a group of men and women whom she characterizes as "a pretty healthy group." But even among those athletes, weight and food are continual concerns. "We have regular discussions about weight and eating," Fulkerson says. "The conversation just sort of wanders over to that.

---

## Anorexia Among Ballet Dancers

The occupational hazards of dancers go beyond pulled hamstrings and paltry paychecks. Anorexia nervosa is claiming careers, and lives, with increasing voracity. Yet as companies prepare for fall seasons, some performers sign contracts agreeing to fines and dismissal if their weight fluctuates.

Marijeanne Liederbach, director of research and education at Harkness Center for Dance Injuries, describes dancers' disordered eating habits as "hideous sabotage," debilitating their artistic potential and livelihood.

"I think every dancer is a potential anorexic," says Donna Boguslav, New York University's director of nursing and associate director of the university health center, who counsels students with health crises. "Every dancer has to deal with weight control. At what point do you cross the line?" Each year Boguslav, herself a former ballet dancer, sees around 20 anorectic dancers, but is sure "there are many more." From ballerinas to cheerleaders to ice skaters, women who make their bodies their instruments—especially in activities that require partnered lifts and acrobatic feats—must limit what they weigh. The last two decades, however, have revealed a pronounced increase in anorexia, which Boguslav attributes to our "retouched fantasy land": today's image-obsessed, heroin-chic society.

Kate Mattingly, *Village Voice*, September 16, 1997.

---

"This morning I did a long run with a friend, a woman who, by any standard, is fit and healthy. When we finished the run, she complained that she was fat and out of shape. That kind of thinking is distorted. When you start to calculate how much should I exercise versus how much do I weigh, rather than how should I best train for this upcoming event, you've got a problem."

It's a struggle Suzi Thibeault knows all too well. Thibeault, known as Suzi T in her ultra-running circles, is not a person one would expect to obsess about food and body weight. Outgoing, full of life and far from fat, her accomplishments include completing the Grand Slam, running five prestigious 100-mile races in one year.

But, she confesses, the anticipation of a run isn't what pushes her out the door to train most days—it's a perceived need to burn the calories from last night's meal. "Undoubtedly, there are many women who run only because they are burning calories," she says. "I'm one of them. There are times I don't want to run, but I need to burn calories. The caloric fight is always on. It's a lifetime fight, and you can't just skip it for a week.

"Even during an ultra, I have trouble eating a powdered doughnut at an aid station. I'd have to make a comment to the aid-station people, something to the effect of, 'I wouldn't ordinarily do this.' And it's silly—to run these distances, you need to fuel your body. I know that. But I still consider certain foods just not allowed."

Suzi T recognizes that her caloric war with herself consumes an exorbitant amount of energy. "I'd go into major depression if I gained 10 pounds right now," she admits. "I obsess about it, absolutely. A day doesn't go by that I don't think about it. If I look at myself in the mirror without clothes on, I'm almost never pleased. Only in August or September, if I've been racing a lot, do I manage to get down to what I consider bathing-suit weight. That lasts about two weeks."

Her discomfort with the body in the mirror, says Suzi T, derives from a cultural emphasis on slimness for women. "I think that, like all women's, my body image is shaped by what I've seen in the entertainment business, on television and in the media." It's Kate Moss, not Jackie Joyner-Kersee, who shapes Suzi T's concept of an ideal body. "We're still talking model caliber rather than running caliber," she says. "This has nothing to do with speed, strength or endurance."

She had worked too hard, too long, for this to happen. Nine miles from the finish line of the Hawaiian Ironman, she lay in the ambulance, barely aware of the IV needle the nurse was trying to insert into her collapsed vein. Her coach held her hand, looking away with each poke. The full moon shimmered overhead; she could see in the distance the glow of lights, like bits of moon that had magically dispersed throughout the night. She listened to the sounds of footsteps and the aid station volunteers' cries of "Gatorade!" "Water!" "Pretzels!" "Cookies!" Offers she had refused all day.

## Compromising Performance and Health

Are women compromising performance and health as they obsess about how much to eat and how much to burn? Absolutely, says Dave Tanner, an exercise physiologist at Indiana University. "If you expend more calories than you consume, the energy needs to come from somewhere, and that will be carbohydrate, fat and protein stores," he says. "Protein will be used as a fuel even though there are still fat stores available." The result: impaired performance and decreased muscle mass and strength.

Taken to an extreme, over-exercise combined with low caloric intake can be life threatening. "You need energy to exercise, and if it isn't there, you digest muscle. The heart is muscle," Tanner explains.

Most of the effects of caloric deprivation, however, are more subtle than a heart attack. Grumpiness, mental dullness and apathy (the brain must have carbohydrates to function, Tanner emphasizes), lack of energy, difficulty completing workouts and slowing times are all classic signs of overtraining—and undereating.

But for most women, the logic of performance and health doesn't weigh heavily in the emotional struggle with food and body. In sports in which thinness is viewed as an advantage, the athlete has difficulty equating poor performance with lack of nutrition. And in sports in which bulk and power are valued, the cultural image of the ideal female body conflicts with the pursuit of optimal athletic performance. Nationally ranked rower Christine Cook attributes her extended fight with bulimia at least in part to the demands of rowing at an elite level. "Rowing at first made my eating disorder worse, although I don't know necessarily if it was just rowing," she says. "With rowing, you're supposed to be tough and big and strong. But I'm also supposed to be a woman and feminine," she says. "That's totally not me—I mean, I'm strong."

Cook's struggle began at 16, when she read an article about bulimia. "I thought, 'Gee, I could do this,'" she remembers. "The woman in the story let it get out of control, but I thought I was different. I could control it." By college, Cook was competing on a national level. "That's when it started to rule my life," she says. "Rowing made my eating disorder much worse. I felt like I had to perform, to stay in the top ranking." The crisis came one morning when, faced with national team testing, Cook found herself bingeing. "I was scared," she recalls. "I wanted a way out. I had gone to bed planning to eat nothing but plain tuna the next day. I ended up eating half a coffee cake first thing in the morning. That's when I realized I could not stop."

Cook was surprised to discover many of her friends had similar troubles. "When I started to talk about it, I was amazed how many people said they had maybe not full-fledged eating disorders but just weird ways of eating." Cook ultimately sought help, admitting herself to Renfrew, an eating-disorders center. Today her goal is to make the Olympic team in 2000.

But many women don't get help because it is not clear to them that they have a problem. How can a woman tell if she does? The first step is to ask what a healthy relationship to food and exercise looks like, Fulkerson says. Such a balance, she explains, is reflected in a healthy, well-rounded life that includes relationships and work outside of an athletic career. "People become so one-dimensional that they cease to look at things like relationships. They isolate themselves," she says. "But a healthy person is happy with life as a whole. Being an athlete is only part of that."

Harrison suggests that many women need to change their approach to diet and exercise. "Dieting is a way to say, 'I'm not okay the way I am, but I will be if I lose X number of pounds.' When we focus on the body as something wrong, we get a lot of cognitive information," she says. "Yet we're still not able to assimilate that information into a nurturing, gentle attitude. Instead, we punish ourselves with it. This is not really about food, but about a discomfort with who we are. As long as we continue to focus on the external, we will use food or body hate as ways to attempt to manage our lives. We need to adopt a more gentle posture toward ourselves."

*"Males represent 8 to 10 percent of all [eating disorder] cases, and . . . the numbers are growing."*

# Men Are at Risk of Eating Disorders

Suzanne Koudsi

In the viewpoint that follows, Suzanne Koudsi challenges the common assumption that eating disorders are exclusively a problem for women. She states that the number of men who suffer from anorexia, bulimia, and binge-eating disorder is higher than typically thought—and appears to be rising. Koudsi claims that eating-disordered men generally fall into two categories: those with psychological problems such as depression, and athletes who become addicted to abnormal eating regimens. Furthermore, she contends, some men develop eating disorders as a result of social pressures to look good. The author is a reporter and editor who writes for *Fortune Magazine*.

As you read, consider the following questions:

1. As cited by Koudsi, how many men suffer from eating disorders?
2. According to the author, what two factors influence the recent growth in the number of males with eating disorders?
3. Why are males with low self-esteem at risk of developing an eating disorder, as stated in the viewpoint?

Reprinted from Suzanne Koudsi, "Behind the Shadows: Males with Eating Disorders," available at http://children.jrn.columbia.edu. Reprinted with permission from the author.

At 5-foot-seven-inches, 168 pounds, this 18-year-old college freshman looks like a typical teenager. He does well in school, plays sports, and has a girlfriend, said Roberto Olivardia, who interviewed him for a study on college-aged men with eating disorders conducted by a team of experts at McLean Hospital in Belmont, MA. But a closer look reveals that the young man's skin is taut against his face and his teeth have no enamel. He vomits three to four times a day. His body is so accustomed to purging that he can open his mouth and rid his stomach of the two gallons of ice cream, one large pizza, and 12 scrambled eggs that he eats on a typical binge.

He grew up in a small town in the Midwest with what he described as a depressed mother, an angry father and an anorexic sister. His bout with bulimia began when he was only 13 years old. This young man is one of a growing number of males diagnosed with what are commonly considered middle-class girls' disorders—bulimia and anorexia.

One day he spotted some flab on his stomach and decided that he needed to lose weight. He tried dieting but when he realized that he couldn't stay away from food, he began bingeing. After hearing a story about sorority sisters sticking their fingers down their throats, he decided to give it a try, and has been self-inducing vomit ever since. Sometimes he throws up so many times that he has nothing left in his stomach but bile.

In 1995 when he volunteered for the McLean male eating disorder study, for which he received $50, he hadn't shared his struggle with anyone but the researchers who interviewed him. And he hadn't sought treatment. Researchers did not follow up with the participants. It is possible that this young man still struggles with his disorder. He is not alone.

## A Growing Problem Among Males

The problem has reached epidemic proportions in America, according to the National Association of Anorexia Nervosa and Associated Disorders (ANAD). Experts agree that males represent 8 to 10 percent of all cases, and that the numbers are growing; though no definitive data exists. Statistics published by ANAD reveal that seven million women and one million men suffer from eating disorders. Eighty-six percent of those men and women report onset of their disorders before the age of 20, and 10 percent report onset at age 10 or younger.

Two factors may influence the recent growth in the number of males with eating disorders. The number of males reporting their disorders has increased in real terms, but awareness has also increased, said Dr. Ira Sacker, director of eating disorders at Brookdale University Hospital Medical Center in Brooklyn, N.Y. In recent years, Sacker has seen more men with eating disorders. He also noted that children are developing eating disorders at younger ages—eating-disordered girls are as young as five and six, and boys are as young as eight and nine.

The ratio between women and men with eating disorders used to be 19 to 1, said Sacker. He has treated more male patients in the past 5 or 6 years, and thinks that the gap between males and females has narrowed to 9 to 1.

"It's not as socially acceptable for a man to have an eating disorder," said Jennifer Carlton, an intake counselor at the Rader Institute, an eating disorder program in Los Angeles, Calif. Women who suffer from eating disorders do not confront as many social consequences as men, said Sacker. Society characterizes skinny men as sick, but doesn't judge thin women. "Anorexia now has become a vogue, it's scary," he said.

## Men's Resistance to Treatment

Society does not accept male anorexia and bulimia. People generally associate these eating disorders with homosexuals and bisexuals, which has made it more difficult for men to seek treatment. It is "not something which any male wants to be identified with," said Sacker. Men also are much more resistant to therapy. Men's resistance is a result of the way in which they were raised. The study conducted by Olivardia, and a team of experts including Dr. Harrison G. Pope, revealed that only 16 percent of their male sample population, which included 50 men, 25 with eating disorders and 25 without, had sought treatment, in comparison with 52 percent of their female sample.

Many men with eating disorders suffer from sexual identity and gender issues, said Dr. Elizabeth Beron at the Program for

Managing Eating Disorders in Manhattan. The link between homosexuality and eating disorders has not been established, although some experts feel that there may be a connection. But according to Pope and Olivardia's study, homosexuality did not appear as a common factor among their sample of eating-disordered men. Homosexuals may be more comfortable admitting their eating disorders and seeking treatment, said Kelly L. Klump, assistant professor of psychology at the University of Minnesota, and if this is the case, any data linking homosexuality to eating disorders may be skewed.

## Two Categories of Men with Eating Disorders

Eating-disordered males generally fall into two categories. Some males develop eating disorders as a result of underlying psychological problems, said Sacker, such as depression, obsessive-compulsive disorder, or anxiety disorder. Others are athletes who become addicted to the habits they form while training for competitive sports. The 18-year-old who lost the enamel on his teeth was a combination of both.

His bulimia was already in full swing when he got to college and joined the wrestling team. He first began using exercise at age 16 as another way to avoid gaining weight—his excessive calorie consumption had finally caught up with him. During wrestling season, his coaches encouraged him to fast for a week to fit into his weight category. He would wear rubber suits and take saunas to rid himself of any extra pounds. After fasting, he and his teammates would binge and build up as much muscle as possible before their meets. He got so good at bingeing and purging that he could lose or gain up to 10 pounds in a matter of days. His bulimia was "one of his friends," said Olivardia. And when he left the Midwest for college, it was the only one he brought with him.

Bulimia and binge eating disorder affect more boys than anorexia, said Olivardia. Younger boys initially suffer from anorexia, said Sacker, but usually it evolves into bulimia.

An eleven-year-old boy lost 30 pounds in two months, said Sacker describing one of his current patients. He exercised two and a half to three hours everyday, doing crunches and running laps. When his parents wouldn't let him outside to exercise, he ran in his bedroom instead. He restricted his diet, and would eat only low-calorie foods—frozen yogurt, salads and apples. The 5-foot-4-inch boy weighed 85 pounds when his parents finally brought him in for treatment.

"They were using him for the relationship," said Sacker. This young boy's parents are divorced, and their son used food to keep his relationship with them under control. "He didn't trust anybody," said Sacker, who worked hard to gain the struggling boy's trust. He acted macho until it came time to stand on the scale. More than a year has passed since he began treatment, and with the help of a nutritionist and therapy, he has managed to keep his weight at a stable 110 pounds, but Sacker still sees the young boy struggling inside.

---

## Eating-Disordered Men Struggle with Greater Distress

Like women with [eating] disorders, men are ashamed of their bodies and are concerned about their sexual attractiveness. . . . However, . . . men struggle with greater distress than women because men shoulder the burden of suffering from a problem incorrectly perceived as affecting only women.

*Psychotherapy Letter*, April 1996.

---

With very young children though, it is difficult to accurately characterize their behavior. A seven-year-old patient of Sacker's refuses to eat. Is he anorexic or is he simply displaying signs of oppositional behavior? This child exhibited enough elements to receive diagnosis as an anorexic, said Sacker, but he was not suffering from classical anorexia.

Some of the growth in eating disorders may be attributed to the fact that many of the adolescents who had eating disorders in the past are now adults, and have passed their symptoms onto their children. Practitioners can trace eating-disordered behavior into families and have found that it is genetic or environmental, said Sacker. Kids learn behaviors by following their parents' example.

Young boys and girls may have similar bouts with eating disorders, although research on young boys is limited. "The factors of the primary eating disorder are very similar," said Dr. Harrison G. Pope Jr., who conducted the study with Olivardia, comparing males to females. In a study of adolescents, Klump found that boys and girls shared the most prominent predictors of disordered eating—intense reactions to stress and a poor ability to distinguish among emotional and physical states, such as sadness and hunger. Dr. Arnold E. Andersen of the University of Iowa Medical School, explains in his work entitled "Eating Disorders in Males: Critical Questions" that the differential rate in eating disorders between men and women stems from psychological and social reasons as opposed to biological reasons.

## Social Pressures to Look Good

"Women have pressures on them to look thin," said Olivardia. But these days with Calvin Klein posting up half-naked pictures of fit men like Marky Mark, men feel more pressure to look good too.

Andersen said that males with low self-esteem may find themselves dieting in an attempt to achieve a stereotypical shape that they hope will affirm their masculinity, give them a sense of control, and command the respect of those around them.

In the last 15 years, men have started to become more self-conscious, said Olivardia. The whole fitness concept is taking hold, said Sacker, "I think male anorexia is more of a 90s thing."

# Periodical Bibliography

The following articles have been selected to supplement the diverse views presented in this chapter. Addresses are provided for periodicals not indexed in the *Readers' Guide to Periodical Literature*, the *Alternative Press Index*, the *Social Sciences Index*, or the *Index to Legal Periodicals and Books*.

| | |
|---|---|
| Liz Applegate | "Running into Trouble," *Runner's World*, April 1998. |
| Concerned Counseling | "Even Moderate Dieting Dangerous," *CCI Journal*, 1998. Available at http://concernedcounseling.com/ccijournal/ed_anorexia_dieting.htm. |
| Jennifer Pitzi Hellwig | "Troubled Teens: Their Struggle with Body Image and Eating Disorders," *HealthGate.com*, November 4, 1996. Available at http://www3.healthgate.com/healthy/parenting/1996/teen-img.asp. |
| Caroline Knapp | "Body Language: Are People with Eating Disorders Desperate for Control or Just Too Sensitive for Their Own Good?" *New York Times Book Review*, January 4, 1998. |
| Linda David Kyle | "Super Heroes and Super Models," *Professional Counselor*, December 1999. Available from PO Box 420235, Palm Coast, FL 32142-0235. |
| Kate Mattingly | "The Thin Pink Line: Dancers' All-Consuming Desires Take Fatal Toll," *Village Voice*, September 16, 1997. |
| Allison Mezzafonte | "Eating Disorders Plague College-Aged Women," *Washington Square News*, October 5, 1999. |
| Benita Mosely | "Striking the Balance," *Women's Sports and Fitness*, May 1997. |
| *National Women's Health Report* | "Adolescents and Eating Disorders," November 1, 1995. |
| Tracy Nesdoly | "The First Bite: Kids' Eating Disorders Are a Serious Concern," *Maclean's*, June 17, 1996. |
| *Women's Health Weekly* | "Too Much Exercise May Put Some Young Women at Risk," June 15, 1998. |

CHAPTER 3

# What Causes Eating Disorders?

# Chapter Preface

A recent study conducted by Renee Goodwin, a researcher at the Northwestern University Medical Center, found that women who had been hospitalized for anorexia or bulimia had less intimate relationships with their fathers than women without eating disorders. Goodwin reported that, among eating-disordered women, "the father-daughter relationship is unsatisfactory, not because the father is never around . . . but when he is around, he monitors her actions while he avoids her emotionally and refuses to accept her." Goodwin also noted that the fathers of women with eating disorders tended to be critical of their daughters' weight and appearance.

Goodwin's findings are part of a growing body of research which suggests that families are a significant influence in whether or not children develop eating disorders. In families where one or both parents are abusive, for example, the child is likely to develop low self-esteem, which is said to be one of the chief predictors of eating disorders. Psychologists also report that children whose parents are unavailable, uncommunicative, or overly critical may have low self-esteem as well.

Experts insist, however, that even supportive families can inadvertently contribute to a child's risk of eating disorders. Some contend that children who experience traumatic events such as divorce or death within the family may develop an eating disorder as a way to maintain a sense of control over one aspect of their lives. In addition, researchers claim, parents who pay too much attention to the appearance of others can unwittingly cause their children to be self-conscious about their bodies. As explained by one writer, "Fathers who make comments about body-size and weight [of] other women, their wives, and their daughters can make the child feel as though the size of her body dictates how much he will love her. . . . A girl with a mother who has disordered eating patterns, who continuously diets or is obsessed with appearance . . . will have a much higher chance of developing an eating disorder later on."

Family attitudes as a cause of eating disorders are discussed in the chapter that follows. The authors in this chapter offer contrasting perspectives on what causes people to develop eating disorders.

*"The acute and constant bombardment of certain images in the media are apparently quite influential in how teens experience their bodies."*

# The Media Contribute to the Incidence of Eating Disorders

Ellen Goodman

Syndicated columnist Ellen Goodman contends in the following viewpoint that the media are partly to blame for the incidence of eating disorders. In her view, the fact that eating disorders more than doubled in the remote South Pacific island of Fiji after Hollywood-produced television shows were introduced there proves that Western media images promote eating disorders. Goodman argues that these images, which define thinness as the cultural ideal, cause women to feel insecure about their bodies.

As you read, consider the following questions:

1. According to Goodman, what are the traditional attitudes about weight gain among Fijians?
2. What evidence does the author provide that Western television contributed to the increase of eating disorders in Fiji?
3. What is the "big success story" of Western entertainment, as stated by the author?

First of all, imagine a place women greet each other at the market with open arms, loving smiles and a cheerful exchange of ritual compliments:

"You look wonderful! You've put on weight!" ·

Does that sound like dialogue from Fat Fantasyland? Or a skit from fat-is-a-feminist-issue satire? Well, this Western fantasy was a South Pacific fact of life. In Fiji, before 1995, big was beautiful and bigger was more beautiful—and people really did flatter each other with exclamations about weight gain.

In this island paradise, food was not only love, it was a cultural imperative. Eating and overeating were rites of mutual hospitality. Everyone worried about losing weight—but not the way we do. "Going thin" was considered to be a sign of some social problem, a worrisome indication the person wasn't getting enough to eat.

The Fijians were, to be sure, a bit obsessed with food; they prescribed herbs to stimulate the appetite. They were a reverse image of our culture. And that turns out to be the point.

## The Arrival of Television

Something happened in 1995. A Western mirror was shoved into the face of the Fijians. Television came to the island. Suddenly the girls of rural coastal villages were watching the girls of "Melrose Place" and "Beverly Hills 90210," not to mention "Seinfeld" and "ER."

Within 38 months, the number of teens at risk for eating disorders more than doubled to 29 percent. The number of high school girls who vomited for weight control went up five times to 15 percent. Worse yet, 74 percent of the Fiji teens in the study said they felt "too big or fat" at least some of the time and 62 percent said they had dieted in the past month.

This before-and-after television portrait of a body image takeover was drawn by Anne Becker, an anthropologist and psychiatrist who directs research at the Harvard Eating Disorders Center. She presented her research at the American Psychiatric Association in May 1999 with all the usual caveats. No, you cannot prove a direct causal link between television and eating disorders. Heather Locklear doesn't cause anorexia. Nor does Tori Spelling cause bulimia.

Fiji is not just a Fat Paradise Lost. It's an economy in transition from subsistence agriculture to tourism, and it's entry into the global economy has threatened many old values.

## A Psychotherapist's View

She sat there in my office, her delicate face obscured by a shield of blond hair, her timid voice just above a whisper: "I want to look like the supermodels. I'm five-foot-nine, so I have the height, but I can't lose the weight. I'd like to look like Cindy Crawford. But I can't get below 140 pounds." She reminded me of a frightened rabbit as her shaky voice grew even quieter, her eyes softened with tears: "I've tried everything, but I just can't."

Time and time again, I hear this confession in the conversations I have with young women. They want to look good in a bathing suit. They want a tight butt. They go on diets and work out every day. They're never thin enough, so they go to unnatural extremes. All they really want is to feel good about themselves in a sea of doubt and turmoil encouraged by a multibillion-dollar-a-year beauty industry. And they think the panacea is to look like a supermodel: perfectly thin, tall, sculpted, and commanding—our cultural epitome of feminine success. I have known hundreds of women who feel justified in their starving, binging and purging, and excessive exercise—their attempts to drain themselves of fat and mold their bodies into the illusions of perfection that pour into their senses from every direction. Of course, despite the money spent, the sweaty hours on the Stairmaster, the deprivation and abuse, most of these women—like most women everywhere—will never look like supermodels. This cruel reality cuts through them like a poison arrow, causing feelings of anger and shame to flood their unforgiving hearts. Initially, many of my patients don't really have lives; their ideas, feelings, and activities all revolve around calories, fat grams, and numbers on a scale.

Jill S. Zimmerman, *Humanist*, January/February 1997.

Nevertheless, you don't get a much better lab experiment than this. In just 38 months, and with only one channel, a television-free culture that defined a fat person as robust has become a television culture that sees robust as, well, repulsive.

All that and these islanders didn't even get "Ally McBeal."

"Going thin" is no longer a social disease but the perceived requirement for getting a good job, nice clothes and fancy cars. As Becker says carefully, "The acute and constant bombardment of certain images in the media are apparently quite influential in how teens experience their bodies."

Speaking of Fiji teens in a way that sounds all-too familiar, she adds, "We have a set of vulnerable teens consuming television. There's a huge disparity between what they see on television and what they look like themselves—that goes not only to clothing, hairstyles and skin color but size of bodies."

In short, the sum of Western culture, the big success story of our entertainment industry, is our ability to export insecurity: We can make any woman anywhere feel perfectly rotten about her shape. At this rate, we owe the islanders at least one year of the ample lawyer Camryn Manheim in "The Practice" for free.

## The Connection Between Image and Illness

I'm not surprised by research showing that eating disorders are a cultural byproduct. We've watched the female image shrink down to Calista Flockhart at the same time we've seen eating problems grow. But Hollywood hasn't been exactly eager to acknowledge the connection between image and illness.

Over the past few weeks since the Columbine High massacre, we've broken through some denial about violence as a teaching tool. It's pretty clear that boys are literally learning how to hate and harm others.

Maybe we ought to worry a little more about what girls learn: To hate and harm themselves.

*"Amazingly thin models are part of a self-enclosed world of aesthetic ideals that has no direct relation to life."*

# The Media Do Not Contribute to the Incidence of Eating Disorders

John Casey

In May 2000, the British Media Association released a report, *Eating Disorders, Body Image, and the Media*, which argues that television images of thinner-than-average women are a "significant cause" of eating disorders. John Casey, a fellow of Caius College in Cambridge and a columnist for the *Evening Standard*, disputes this notion in the subsequent viewpoint. He maintains that the thin women featured on television and in fashion magazines represent an aesthetic ideal that has little influence on how real women live.

As you read, consider the following questions:

1. How does Casey characterize the "realm of fashion and catwalks"?
2. What is the "anxiety game," as defined by the author?

Excerpted from John Casey, "Thin Advice from Thick Doctors," *Evening Standard*, May 31, 2000. Reprinted with permission from the *Evening Standard*.

Thin models, on the catwalk and on television, have become a mortal danger to intellectually challenged young girls. That seems to be the view of the British Medical Association [BMA] which has commissioned a weighty report on the situation. Dr Vivienne Nathanson, launching the report—*Eating Disorders, Body Image and the Media*—said that its conclusion is that images of thinner-than-average women are a "significant cause" of eating disorders such as anorexia nervosa and bulimia.

Dr Nathanson went on: "Research has also found that most female characters on TV are thinner than average women. The images of slim models in the media are in marked contrast to the body size and shape of most children and young women, who are becoming increasingly heavier."

Curiously enough, even without the benefit of the "research" commissioned (at presumably some expense) by the BMA, I had already formed the impression that women on television and the catwalk tend to be not only slimmer but prettier than the ones you see on the street. I had assumed that this helped explain how they got there in the first place, for years of reflection have convinced me that we prefer to contemplate good-looking men and women rather than nerds and frumps.

It also struck me as a bit strange that Dr Nathanson was worried about the influence of the slim beauties on impressionable girls just at a time when children and women are becoming "heavier"—presumably polite-speak for "obese".

Nevertheless, there are (we are told) 60,000 people in the United Kingdom with eating disorders, 90 per cent of them young women. Presumably a healthy (if that is the right word) proportion of them are the fatties, for whom to aspire to be more like Naomi Campbell can do nothing but good.

Otherwise, the most obvious thing to say, surely, is that only the dimmest among us will mistake the realm of fashion and catwalks for the real world.

## A World of Fantasy

Everything about it marks it out as a world of fantasy, of clothes that no one in their right mind would dream of wearing and of models who are scarcely more real than Giacometti sculptures.

But the BMA apparently wants to keep the world safe for those few dimwits who do not realise that these amazingly thin models are part of a self-enclosed world of aesthetic ideals that has no direct relation to life.

There is nothing new about this. The ancient Greeks worshipped gods, each of whom represented some idealised aspect of human nature. Apollo was the majestic artist and prophet, noble and beautiful to look at; but not especially muscular. Hercules represented the ideal of muscular youth, and Poseidon—god of the sea and of earthquakes—strength in mature age.

But the Greeks were not foolish enough to believe that anyone could actually resemble these ideals, let alone the average man.

True, Alexander the Great and, later, Christ were probably modelled on Apollo but both of them were thought of as divine. I suppose our problem is that we are less sophisticated than our forebears were about conventions assumed in representing the human form. There is no need to believe that Nefertiti, willowy-looking wife of the heretical Pharaoh, Akhenhaton, was as flawlessly beautiful as she is portrayed in the famous bust of her in Berlin.

But we can assume that this is an ideal version of a genuinely beautiful woman.

If you look at the fleshy, voluptuous reclining nudes of Rubens, it would be naïve to think that these pictures might have had the effect of encouraging young women of the 17th century to stuff themselves with fatty foods.

## The Difference Between Art and Reality

It is true that Rubens was responding to a sexual ideal different from the modern one—one that stressed mature female voluptuousness over androgynous frailty. But Rubens's patrons understood the difference between art and reality.

The odd thing is that in countries such as Egypt and India where a preference for the full female form is still so well-established that mothers have traditionally fattened up their daughters to make them marriageable, and where men still look for plumpness in women, wafer-thin Western film stars are nevertheless extremely popular.

Contrary to what the BMA seems to assume, most people still understand the role of conventions. For years the splendid soprano, Rita Hunter, appeared as Brunhilde in productions of Wagner's Ring at the Coliseum. Brunhilde is supposed to be a fiery, athletic warrior goddess. Miss Hunter was so ample that some seconds seem to elapse from the first manifestation of her bosom from the wings to the full appearance of the rest of her.

## The Thin Ideal Bears Little Relation to Reality

It is extraordinary that women such as actresses Calista Flockhart and Courtney Cox, who are regarded as excessively thin, may be criticised for their appearance but would not be damned were they overweight. And this is so, despite obesity now being regarded in the United States as the most significant health problem among children. . . .

Far more people . . . are likely to suffer the consequences of being overweight than underweight. What this information suggests is that the thin ideal, whether promoted by fashion or any other industry, bears little relation to reality. While eating disorders are obviously matters of serious concern, their origins are clearly much more complex than teenage girls looking at the fashion pages of glossy magazines.

*Irish Times*, Saturday, June 24, 2000. Available at http://www.ireland.com/newspaper/newsfeatures/2000/0624/newfeatures7.htm.

It was out of the question that she could ever vault onto a horse. But because Miss Hunter was a magnificent, dramatic singer and not absolutely terrible as an actress, you soon came to discount her physical appearance and see her as a heroine.

For women to be fat or thin is entirely a matter of style.

There is nothing morbid or unnatural in societies that prefer one extreme or the other. A friend of mine was in a seedy cafe in Morocco with a German couple. The wife was stupendously obese. The pair were being regarded with some intensity by a small group of Moroccan Arabs who later approached the husband.

How much would he take for his wife? "She is the most beautiful woman we have ever seen."

I suppose questions of health do arise in extreme cases. A

woman who literally resembled a Hottentot Venus (they really did exist) with pathologically overdeveloped breasts and buttocks would presumably have as short a life as a Sumo wrestler. But in matters of erotic beauty and, generally, of physical style, fantasy is all.

## The Anxiety Game

Dr Nathanson and the BMA are simply playing, in a routine sort of way, the anxiety game. They seize upon the harm that the dimmest members of our society might, just possibly, do to themselves if they cannot distinguish between fantasy and reality, and then use it as a solemn excuse for meddlesome nannying.

Luckily the whole, weird world of fashion is far too dominated by vested interests for them to have the slightest chance of spoiling the fun.

*"Having a mother who is obsessed with being thin and who diets regularly is considered one of the risk factors for the development of an eating problem in an adolescent girl."*

# Family Attitudes Play a Role in the Development of Eating Disorders

Sharlene Hesse-Biber

Sharlene Hesse-Biber states in the following viewpoint that young women who believe in the cultural ideal for body image—which values extreme slenderness—are at risk of developing eating disorders. According to Hesse-Biber, the influence of the family is a major factor in determining whether women accept or reject cultural ideals of thinness. Families who convey the message that to be thin is to be loved may cause their female children to develop problematic relationships with food.

As you read, consider the following questions:

1. What powerful message is conveyed by society's popular culture, according to Hesse-Biber?
2. As explained by the author, how did Barbara's family contribute to the development of her eating disorder?
3. How do mothers' attitudes about body image and eating influence their daughters, in the author's view?

Keep young and beautiful.
It's your duty to be beautiful.
Keep young and beautiful,
If you want to be loved.

Don't fail to do your stuff
With a little powder and a puff.
Keep young and beautiful,
If you want to be loved.

If you're wise, exercise all the fat off.
Take it off over here, over there.
When you're seen anywhere with your hat off,
Wear a marcelled wave in your hair.

Take care of all those charms,
And you'll always be in someone's arms.
Keep young and beautiful,
If you want to be loved.

The words of a popular song echo a powerful message in our culture—that only the beautiful and the thin are valued and loved. Reiterated by families, peers, and the school environment, this notion is taken seriously by many young women. So seriously, in fact, that anorexia nervosa (obsession with food, starvation dieting, severe weight loss) and bulimia (compulsive binge eating, followed by purging through self-induced vomiting or laxatives) occur ten times more frequently in women than in men. These syndromes usually develop during adolescence and, until recently, were more prevalent among upper- and upper-middle class women.

These behaviors carry long-term physical risks, ranging from tooth enamel destroyed by stomach acid, to malnutrition, to organ damage, to death. Anorexia is one of the few psychiatric disorders with a significant mortality rate. The American Anorexia/Bulimia Association estimates that 10% of those diagnosed with anorexia may die. Bulimia is thought to be four to five times more common than anorexia, but is more difficult to detect. Bulimics are usually secretive about their gorge-and-purge episodes, and since there is often nothing about their external appearance to alert anyone to the presence of the disorder, the condition goes undiagnosed unless they seek help themselves. The number of women dying from bulimia is hard to estimate, but bulimia can have serious medical consequences, like gastrointestinal damage. The emotional toll of these disorders can include feelings of despair, self-loathing, guilt, depression, low self-esteem, and an inability to conduct normal relationships.

In recent years, the topic of eating disorders has emerged from the realm of clinical case studies in scholarly journals to a place of prominence in the public eye. As is often the case, the afflictions of celebrities have helped pave the way for a greater focus on a widespread problem. The starvation-related death of singer Karen Carpenter, and the confessions of Jane Fonda and Princess Diana that they suffered from bulimia, have received copious coverage and created a climate of acceptance. . . .

When I surveyed the college women in my sample, I wasn't surprised that 77% of them chose the cultural model as their desired image, and 23% the medical model. But I was interested in the link between the culture's demands for slenderness and the rise in eating disorders. I wanted to know if adhering to these norms might make these young women more vulnerable to developing eating problems. So I administered the Eating Attitudes Test, a standard measure of eating disorders. The results gave me the connection I was looking for. Of the women who followed the cultural ideal, *24% scored in the abnormal range,* compared to only 8% of the medical model followers. In addition, almost half of the cultural ideal followers (47%) compared to only about one-fourth of the medical followers (26%) reported significant to extreme concern about their body weight; 34% said they felt anxious, depressed, or repulsed by their bodies, compared with only 25% of medical model followers. The link was clear: *those women who believed in the cultural definition of body image were more at risk for the development of eating difficulties.*

If we were to rely only on traditional psychology to explain the current near-epidemic increase in eating disorders among college women, we would have to assume an increase in the underlying mental and emotional features that produce such symptoms. There is a big difference, however, between disorderly eating patterns and clinically defined eating disorders. College students in my sample displayed many of the *behavioral* symptoms associated with anorexia and bulimia. In order to live up to the cultural mandate of thinness, they engaged in calorie restriction, chronic dieting, bingeing and purging, and the use of diuretics or laxatives. Some also used extreme exercise to control their weight, becoming overly dependent on a rigid workout schedule to make them feel "alive." Yet, they did *not* exhibit the full constellation of psychological traits usually associated with an eating disorder, such as maturity fears, interpersonal distrust, and perfectionism. Their behavior mimicked anorexia and bulimia without the accompanying psychological profiles. Some researchers refer to this pattern as "imitative anorexia," "subclinical eating disorders," or "weight preoccupation." I refer to it as *culturally induced* eating; a pattern of eating disordered symptoms in otherwise psychologically "normal" women. Disorderly eating and obsession with food is a widely accepted way to deal with weight and body image issues. *It is normative behavior for women who are part of the Cult of Thinness.*

## The Consequences of Disordered Eating

But sometimes these strategies have unintended consequences. Severe food restriction over time may trigger an uncontrollable binge, which the dieter feels necessary to then purge. Women who tamper with their body's natural metabolism through dieting may find they gain weight on fewer calories. Excessive exercise can lead to injury or burnout, or even halt menstruation. All of this fosters constant weight preoccupation and an overconcern with body image. These behaviors may lead to depression, or develop into long term eating disorders with their accompanying psychopathology.

There were indeed women in my research sample who would be classified with an eating disorder. Frequently they were women who had a history of severe trauma—sexual abuse, family dysfunction, and/or physical abuse. They used eating as a mechanism to cope and to empower. In a sense, manipulating food intake is one culturally approved way that women can gain some influence over their environment. Control of their own bodies is a substitute for control over their economic, political, and social lives. For example, rejecting food may send a powerful message to a problematic family. Overeating may be a safe way to soothe emotional pain.

Linda, one of my interview subjects who was bulimic, told me:

> Food is nurturing for me. Over the past six months, since I've been dealing with sexual abuse issues, my bulimia has disappeared to the point where I can go for a month without having a problem. When I do have a problem, I know what I'm doing with the food. It's nurturance, and I understand that, at the time, and that's when I give in to it. You know, you can't fight your battles on every front all the time. I realize I'm giving in to this bulimia, but if that is what I need right now to take care of me, that's all right.

Purging may be a means for some women to vent the anger and frustration they feel in dealing with their home environment, sexual abuse, or mistreatment from society. They may experience secondary advantages such as weight loss, but this may not be their primary motivation. Some women may feel an important sense of control in the decision to eat or not eat. Food is a means for self-expression and power.

Kim, an anorectic, expressed the difference between disorderly eating and eating disorders.

> I think my issue was wanting to control my life. There were a lot of family issues and personal issues that were going on in my life freshman year of high school and I just started with a diet. I suddenly decided I wouldn't eat more than 300 calories. My parents had gotten separated freshman year, my dad remarried that summer and my mom had gotten cancer. There was a tremendous amount of anger, pain that I didn't deal with. I have two brothers and a sister, and everyone took a different route to deal with all of these things that were happening—trauma, basically. And I was always an internal person. My sister is quicker and lets out anger, and I didn't do that as much. So I just sort of went into my own little world, I think. And then that world became totally about eating and weight.

Kim used food to express her anger and sadness. She acted out her personal trauma through her body, and adjusted her food intake as a way to exert some power over her own small corner of the world. In a way, she appropriated our culture's mandate that women "look thin" and turned it into a drastic coping mechanism.

Unlike Kim and Linda, the majority of women in my sample used disorderly eating primarily as a way to maintain a culturally correct body image. Such eating behavior, risky though it may be, is considered "normal."

## The Family and the Thinness Message: Mothers, Fathers, and Siblings

The family is a child's first interpreter of the larger world. Some families repeat the cultural values of thinness, others modify the message. Barbara's case is an extreme example of how parents can amplify the message that to be beautiful is to be loved. This message dominated her outlook on life, and contributed to the development of a full-blown eating disorder.

Barbara was about to turn 20 when I interviewed her for this book. I had known her for almost two years and I'd had an ongoing dialogue with her concerning her weight and body image, and the chronic problems she had with anorexia and bulimia. From appearances, Barbara seemed a happy, well-adjusted college co-ed. She was not overweight, but she did want to lose a few pounds and spent considerable time working out at the college gym. Her hidden history of anorexia started in seventh grade. Her bulimic symptoms began in the ninth grade and continued throughout her high school and college years.

Barbara's parents had had serious marital problems for a long time. Her father, toward whom she felt a great deal of ambivalence, had very high standards of feminine beauty. She grew up observing how difficult it was for her mother to live up to her father's expectations of the ideal woman.

> For my father, a woman has to look perfect. She has no brains. My mother has to go to my dad's functions and she has to just sit there with a smile on her face and look great at parties. My father loves it that his wife looks so much younger than everybody else. . . . I don't think they were ever friends. They were just kind of physically attracted to each other. She does everything to please my father. She would go on a diet for my father. She colors her hair for my father. She got fake contacts for my father. She lies out in the sun all summer. That's all my dad wants to do, be as tan as he can, and she wants to be as tan as she can for him. . . . And, oh

my god, my father would get in fights, would not even talk to my mother for like a week, because her toenails weren't painted and she was wearing open-toed shoes!

Barbara did not escape her father's criticism of her own body. As a preadolescent she was taller than the other girls in her class and this made her feel "big." "When I was little my dad always used to make fun of me. I was never fat, just tall, but he used to pinch my stomach and say 'Barbie, you got a little rubber tire in there.'"

## The Role of Family Dynamics

Family dynamics, according to [Amy] Tuttle [a nutrition therapist at the Renfrew Center in Philadelphia], often contribute to the development of an eating disorder. "Some people with eating disorders come from enmeshed families where emotional, relational and physical space boundaries may be too blurry. This 'enmeshment' inhibits independence and the development of a separate self," says Tuttle. A prominent theory about eating disorders—that the person with the eating disorder is trying to gain some measure of control in her life—is consistent with this type of family structure. For some people, the act of dieting itself provides an illusion of control.

*Food Insight*, January/February 1997. Available at http://ificinfo.health.org/insight/eatingawry.htm.

So Barbara stopped eating in the seventh grade. "I lost so much weight they were going to send me to a hospital, because I refused to eat. I wanted to be thin and I loved it. I ate the minimum, a little bowl of cereal for breakfast. I wouldn't eat a dessert. I remember my father forcing me to eat a bowl of ice cream. I was crying and he said, 'You're going to eat this, you know,' which was funny because he always used to call me fat. I used to lie down every night on my bed and love to see how my hip bones would stick out so much.

"When my father said, 'You're even skinner than your sister,' I was so happy inside. It was like an accomplishment, finally for once in my life I was thinner than my sister. I remember going shopping with her to get jeans. I tried on size zero and they fell off. It was the best feeling I'd ever had in my entire life. I went back to school weighing under 90 pounds and I was about 5 feet 6 inches. I loved competitive sports, so when I couldn't play tennis anymore because I was fainting, I started eating. I started noticing that I could eat so much and get on the scale and I wouldn't even gain any weight because I was playing so much tennis. My eating was normal during that period, the eighth grade. But I wouldn't eat in front of anyone."

Then she started bingeing and vomiting. "It was awful. It was the worst feeling. You know you are about to throw up but you have to get the last bite in. I don't understand how, when you are going to throw up, you're walking right to the bathroom and you're still shoving food in. My bingeing would only happen when I was alone, before my parents came home."

Barbara's eating problems continued into her college years. She described a typical binge:

> I still binge and I always do the exact same thing. I put on my backpack and go to the local food store. I don't want to talk to anybody. I always get cookies, cake, and ice cream because it is easy to throw up. Chipwiches, brownies, sundaes. Once I stole from the cafeteria because I was too embarrassed to buy it. The minute I get back to my room, I lock the door and turn on the music. I can't throw up in my bathroom be-cause other girls will hear so I turn on the music and throw up in my room. I'll get a garbage bag from downstairs first. It's so gross. After I throw up I feel awful—it can be so ex-hausting all you do is fall asleep.

## No Escaping the Pressure to Be Thin

For Barbara, there was no escaping the pressure to be thin and attractive "because that's what my father thinks and likes. I guess I want to live up to his standard." Yet she knew how devastating this has been for her mother and how rocky a relationship her parents had.

"I always said to my mom that I'd never want to marry someone like Dad. I don't want what happened to my mom to happen to me. He just wants my mother to look young for the rest of her life. He doesn't want her to go gray. The big joke in my house now is that my mother's going through menopause and she just cries all the time. And my dad is like, 'You're so old'. And my mother is just devastated. She looks a lot younger, but my dad always tells her she looks old. She doesn't look old. A lot of people ask if she's my sister. And I mean, she has to wear bikinis. She doesn't want to. She always has to wear full face makeup on the beach, because you can't show like any blemishes, or anything. You have to look perfect. It always drove my father crazy that my sister and I don't wear makeup.

"My father is definitely there when we go shopping. He always looks through women's fashion magazines, cuts out photos for us. 'I think you should get this outfit, this outfit.' I mean we have piles of these stupid pictures. When my mom and dad came up to visit me at college, I had to change to go out to dinner, because I wasn't wearing a skirt. I thought I looked fine, but he was embarrassed.

"I get angry, but then again, it's the way I've always been brought up. My dad would say, 'Yeah, we might be kind of crazy, but look how much we've given you.' I was always angry at my mom for never saying anything. She always knew I was right, but she would never say anything. She was always such a wimp.

"My dad has never seen divorce as an alternative. He thinks, you get married, it's for life. I know inside he loves my mother more than anybody. It's weird. He can't show it, but I know he does. When I was growing up I remember always listening to them fight. When my mother would be crying, I would say, 'Why don't you just leave him?' and my mother's reason was, 'I like my financial life style. I like going to Europe every year. I like having a summer house. I like having my summers off. If I get divorced I can't have any of that.'"

## Bulimia as a Coping Mechanism

Part of Barbara's response to these pressures was bulimia. She used compulsive eating to numb her anxiety and anger, and purging to relieve her dread of being fat and unloved.

She had also begun to develop some of the psychological symptoms that are classic for women with eating problems, like maturity fears. In many ways Barbara was afraid of growing up and facing what her mother experienced as an adult married woman. She could see how women are devalued in society. As Nancy Chodorow says, "The flight from womanhood is not a flight from uncertainty about feminine identity but from knowledge about it. Instead, she loved playing the kid role, making up fantasy tales and playing on the swings in the playground. As she put it, "I was always the goof ball. You know, like I never grew up. The night before I left for college my mother said I didn't have to go. She was like, "You're my baby, I don't care if you don't go to college."

It is clear that there are a variety of pathological issues within Barbara's family, but Barbara's eating problems cannot be fully understood without an awareness of their setting. The assumptions of our culture are evident in her father's demands that his daughters and wife look thin and perfect.

It is impossible to point out any one factor in the family environment that would explain how families induct their daughters into the Cult of Thinness. Some parents go out of their way to *avoid* emphasizing body image issues with their daughters. However, the college women I interviewed were quick to point out the little ways their families passed on the cultural message.

## How Mothers' Attitudes Influence Daughters

Mothers are crucial brokers of the wider cultural norms. Some research studies note how a mother's attitudes about her own body image and eating behavior influence her daughter. Having a mother who is obsessed with being thin and who diets regularly is considered one of the risk factors for the development of an eating problem in an adolescent girl.

Pamela gave me an extreme example of how a mother's concerns led her daughter to take a very dim view of her own body image and self-esteem:

> My mom would always tell me that I was very chunky. She's 5'1" and weighs about 100 pounds, so she always fits into size two and four clothes. And here I am, I can't get fit a piece of her clothing on my elbow. I'm the fat one, her fat daughter. I don't want to be near her. She always looks good, has to have the nicest clothes. I just feel very obese next to her.

Through her chronic dieting, Betty's mother conveyed an important message to her daughter when she was growing up. Later on, in college, Betty mimicked her mother's attitudes about weight and eating issues in her own way, by becoming bulimic.

My mom considers herself overweight. She always dieted, trying all those new, different diets, and I'd go on them with her. She tried diet books and the new rotation diet. She'll fluctuate, losing some but then she'll gain it back. Right now she's at a point where she says, 'I'd like to be thinner, but your dad and I like to eat.' And they go out to eat often and it's hard to stay on a diet. So she's coming to accept it, but I think she'd still like to lose weight.

Betty described how her mother always prepared big meals. "My brothers and father liked to eat. We always had a lot of food on the table and we usually had seconds. My grandfather would reward us for cleaning our plates. Even now I feel like I have to eat everything on my plate, even if I'm not hungry."

Not surprisingly, Betty was always very conscious of her weight and body image. "I have this little chart that I try to follow. It has your height and your build, if you're medium or small boned. It has how many calories are in anything you eat. My mom put it in my stocking at Christmas."

When she was a college freshman she gained enough weight to prompt her father's remark that she was getting a "little chubby." Her bulimia started during her sophomore year, after a Christmas party.

I made myself throw up. I had been drinking at the party and I just ate out of control. I couldn't believe that I had eaten all that stuff. It was cookies mainly. I never thought I could throw up, and then I tried and it worked. I tried so hard to keep my weight down and I was 115 and that's where I wanted to stay. And then I'd creep back up. To get all the food out of my stomach, especially that high-calorie food, I threw up.

I didn't have time to join a fitness club and I tried to run, but I didn't feel like I was exercising. I could just feel myself gaining weight and that made me nervous and I felt like if I didn't have time to exercise, then throwing up was kind of the answer. I tried dieting and I wouldn't eat for awhile, and then I would eat a lot. I can't go a whole day without eating. I think that's a major reason why I throw up too. Because I like to eat."

Trapped by two conflicting messages—"Be Thin" and "Eat"—Betty used bulimia as a solution.

Mothers can also serve to modulate cultural norms of thinness and alleviate some of the pressures young girls may feel. Joanna, who is not overweight, described her mother's attitude.

> My mother, all she wants is that I'm happy. I can weigh 500 pounds as long as I'm happy. Her focus was always on my health, not so much with my appearance. So her comments were more towards that positive support. Very rarely do I remember her giving anything like negative comments about how I looked. It was encouraging. My mother would say stuff like 'You have a beautiful face, you have beautiful hands.' She'd focus on individual qualities about me.

## The Role of Fathers

For the most part, the fathers of the women in my study were silent about their daughters' body image. Barbara's father (above) was unusual. So was Marsha's—her father wanted her to be thin and have perfect grades. "He always looked at us as showpieces. That's how he thought other people saw us." Her mother was very overweight when she was growing up; it was Marsha's father who told her she was fat. "I was three years old when my dad started calling me fat. He used to sing me a song, 'I don't want her, you can have her, she's too fat for me,' and I used to cry every time. It was terrible. He was repulsed by my weight, just as he was by my mother's."

Jessica's father was more typical: "I can't recall my father saying much about my appearance. Like if I put on a skirt he'd say: 'Oh, you *do* have legs' and he joked about it. Never anything negative."

Helen's father was also quiet. On special occasions he might say a word or two: "It was one of those things where if you bought a new dress for a prom, and you tried it on for him he'd say, 'Oh, that looks great' or 'very nice' or whatever. But as far as day to day, he'd never say anything. To tell you the truth I don't think he would even know what to say because that's not the type of question that he'd answer. He'd think, 'What kind of a question is that, 'How do I look?''"

The role of siblings as mediators of cultural values has even less documentation. It is clear, however, that older siblings can be an important influence on how young girls think about their bodies.

Judith's older sister made fun of her weight. "My older

sister teased me because I was larger than all my siblings. I was three or four inches taller than even my older sister. And I think I was also bigger. I started developing earlier. She used to say 'You're a fatso.' It used to get me mad, but then when I looked at myself, I would think, 'But, I'm not fat!'"

Sibling rivalry led Katy's family to label each other according to certain body features, and hers was her weight.

One of my brothers was little, and we called him Little Bit. Jeffrey had buck teeth, Judy had freckles. My other sister had a funny nose. My older sister we called the Prima Donna because she's always putting everything on and looks so nice. Everyone had a label. My five brothers and sisters would make pig noises around me. At the time it really hurt my feelings because I'm a very sensitive person. I really was upset but my parents really didn't know I was. It bothered me that they never really said "Katy may be heavy, but she's a person, she's your sister, don't talk to her like that." They never said that and I think I resent it to this day.

*"Individuals who diet are eight times more likely to develop eating disorders."*

# Dieting Can Cause Eating Disorders

Carol Emery Normandi and Laurelee Roark

Carol Emery Normandi and Laurelee Roark, authors of *It's Not About Food*, from which the subsequent viewpoint is taken, contend that dieting is a major cause of eating disorders. Women who starve themselves to lose weight often develop a preoccupation with eating, which in turn places them at risk of developing eating disorders. The authors argue that the prevalence of dieting among women is caused by social pressures that encourage women to strive for abnormally thin bodies.

As you read, consider the following questions:

1. What evidence do the authors provide that diets do not work?
2. How do the authors support their claim that young women are obsessed with food and weight?
3. What societal pressures do women face, as stated by Normandi and Roark?

*I have been a compulsive eater ever since high school, when I became aware of messages that made me feel my body was not acceptable the way it was. I was a teenage model in the sixties. When Twiggy came on the fashion scene, we were all urged to weigh less than one hundred pounds. At a time when my body was still developing calcium for my bones and teeth, hormones for my reproductive system, and cells for my brain, I was eating less than a thousand calories a day. I came to believe that if I would just lose a few pounds my body and my self would then be accepted. Somehow, because I didn't have the "perfect" body, I got the message that my whole being was defective. Instead of having a problem—a defective body—I became the problem—a defective person.*

*I would have tried anything to get thin and stay thin. I believed that if I could be thin, then I could be happy, joyous, and free. When I was fat and bingeing, I was convinced I would be happy if I was thin and dieting. When I was thin and dieting I was terrified that soon I would be fat and bingeing again. Years of my life went by in this pattern, some of them only highlighted by what I weighed or what diet I was on. My level of self-hatred and despair was unbearable. I thought all that was wrong with me could be measured by pounds. Thinness was my god and I was on a spiritual quest. I sought refuge from pain in the churches of Weight Watchers, Jenny Craig, and Dr. Atkins diets. I was looking outside myself to fix the ache inside me.*

*—Laurelee*

Millions of American women will find the above story familiar. The struggle with dieting, loathing our bodies, and looking outside ourselves to feel better has become an integral part of so many of our daily lives. To get through a day without worrying about what to eat, how it will make us fat, or what our body looks like, is a difficult challenge for many women and men. Thinness through dieting has become our cultural obsession and for many has evolved into a reason for being.

## Obsessed with Dieting

Even though 98 percent of all dieters regain their weight back within five years, and 95 percent within two years, Americans continue to be obsessed with dieting. In 1990 it was estimated that the weight-loss business made $32 billion in 1989 and was expected to exceed $50 billion by 1995 (*US News & World Report*, 1990). Pick a day and you'll find more than one fourth of American women on a diet, with as many as half of them "cheating," completing, or beginning a diet cycle all over again (Roberta Seid, *Never Too Thin*).

As Americans are spending their valuable time and resources on finding the perfect body through dieting, they are actually placing themselves at risk of developing an eating disorder. Research indicates that self-imposed dieting can result in eating binges and in preoccupation with food and eating (Polivy, *Journal of the American Dietetic Association*, 1996) and that individuals who diet are eight times more likely to develop eating disorders (L.K. George Hsu, *Eating Disorders*).

Many women have no idea how insidious their eating disorders will become when they start dieting and starving themselves. They then often yo-yo up and down the scale. Their life becomes consumed by their weight and the desire to stay ultrathin. They have become addicted to dieting and have no idea what their natural weight is.

> *I started dieting when I was thirteen. As I look back now, I can see that I had feelings of insecurity that were surfacing as I struggled with relationships, my identity, and my sexuality. Back then it just felt like I was too fat. As my body began to change from a normal, undeveloped child to a rounder, curvier woman, I held on to the ideals I saw in the media of the very thin, tall, hard bodies that defined beauty. My body was wrong. All my emotional struggles and insecurities became placed on my body. The first day I put myself on a diet, I stopped listening to the wisdom and truth of my own body. I began instead the pattern of forcing myself to conform to cultural standards that were impossible for me to obtain. My soul was crying out for love, for reassurance, security, and emotional soothing during a very overwhelming, confusing period in my life. The only way I knew how to soothe myself was to eat. The only way I knew how to be accepted was to diet. My voice, my cry for help became buried under the obsession and compulsion of dieting and bingeing, bingeing and purging.*

> —*Carol*

## Eating Disorders Start Early

Eating disorders start early and for those afflicted it doesn't stop easily. According to the National Association of Anorexia Nervosa and Associated Disorders (ANAD), 86 percent of victims of eating disorders report the onset of their illness by age twenty, with 33 percent reporting onset between the ages of eleven to fifteen. The way our youth have incorporated this obsession with food and weight into the development of self-esteem is frightening. In a survey done by Mellin, Irwin, and Scully (1982), 65 percent of eleven-year-old girls worry that they are too fat, and approximately 80 percent of eleven-year-old girls reported dieting behaviors. It is also estimated that 90 percent of high school junior and senior adolescents diet regularly. The Council on Size and Weight Discrimination reports that young girls are more afraid of becoming fat than they are of nuclear war, cancer, or losing their parents.

The enormity of the problem cannot be fully understood until we acknowledge it in terms of lost and wasted lives. According to the American Anorexia/Bulimia Association, one out of every one hundred teenage girls becomes anorexic, and 10 percent of them may die as a result. Over a thousand women die every year of anorexia. This figure does not include bulimics or compulsive eaters who die as a result of their eating disorder.

Of all of the eating-disorder patients, 90 percent are female. To be a woman in our culture is to be on a diet, worried about weight, or on the verge of an eating disorder. To be a woman is to hate our bodies and to strive for an ideal body that is unattainable and unnatural for most of us. Fashion models, who embody the ideal of feminine beauty, weigh about 23 percent less than the national average woman. We now have the youngest, skinniest, and most anorexic models that we have had for twenty years. Every month, in any beauty magazine, one can see mere children, or at least childlike bodies, selling clothes being pitched to much more mature women.

## The Devastating Impact of Culture

How can we continue to ignore the devastating impact our culture is having on our women and girls? A recent study showed that social comparison and societal factors were significant predictors of body dissatisfaction and eating disturbance (*International Journal of Eating Disorders*, March 1996). Another study showed that the amount of time watching soaps and movies encouraged body dissatisfaction, and the watching of music videos led to a drive for thinness (*Interna-*

*tional Journal of Eating Disorders*, September 1996).

In a 1984 *Glamour* magazine survey of 33,000 women by Drs. Wayne and Susan Wooley of the University of Cincinnati College of Medicine, 75 percent of eighteen- to thirty-five-year-old American women felt "fat," but only 25 percent of them were defined as medically overweight. In a culture in which the feminine is devalued, most women are ashamed of those parts of the body that contribute to the female shape—their stomachs, hips, thighs, and breasts. The shame is strong enough to drive them to "improve" their appearance by cosmetic surgery. In fact, it's estimated that 250,000 liposuctions are performed every year in the United States. The very young age that most girls are pressured to start seriously dieting—adolescence—is when their bodies turn decidedly feminine, suddenly departing, quite naturally, from the ideal that most models represent. So many adolescent girls find that their ideal body shape is the shape of a boy: flat, toned stomach, concave chest, and slim hips.

*All my life I heard, "you have such a pretty face." That statement almost killed me. I would have done anything to lose weight and I did do lots of crazy things. I started taking diet pills (speed) in order to lose weight. I became bulimic and threw up after every meal to lose weight. I have taken laxatives and had colonics. I had urine shots from a doctor and was put on a fast by a medical group. Nothing worked for very long. I always returned to my normal size. Big. But recently I went back to visit my family in Europe and met with my women cousins and aunts. I saw my own body type and realized that I had been trying to be a size that just wasn't natural for my heritage.*

—*Julie*

In America we have racism, ageism, sexism, and sizism. Though it is not very acceptable to call people ethnic names or to refer to someone as old, nothing stops the media, the friends, or the families from commenting on someone's weight. Names are called, jobs are lost, marriages break up, and everyone "understands," particularly if the person is "too fat." An overweight woman walking down the street has no defense against the looks and the raised eyebrows. This levies a heavy toll on these women. Julie's story is an example of a woman whose genetic heritage determined her body size. Yet we have no room for such individualized characteristics in our society. Even genetically large women may try to force their bodies to conform to the arbitrary ideals of society. Even if they are not "overweight" according to their genetic heritage, they are *judged* to be; many times women gain weight in order to protect themselves from the attacks. It can become a vicious cycle. The same weight is gained and lost hundreds of times. Not only does the person's weight wildly fluctuate but with each diet their total body weight may very well be inching up.

## The Pressure Women Face

Women in this culture have an enormous pressure on them to be perfect. This pressure is put on them early on and is maintained until the day they die. Somewhere along the line many internalize the pressure. The pressure builds and builds, until it is overwhelming, even for the strongest of the strong, the brightest of the bright, and the prettiest of the pretty. Like a cancer that stalks the cells, the push to be sexier, younger, thinner, smarter, nicer, and more successful than everybody else, eats away at a woman's soul. Finally her self-esteem, her self-will, and her self-control are gone, and soon she has no self at all. The expectation to be superwoman and superthin is undermining a whole generation of women. Dieting and obsessing about food, weight, and body image represent the *norm* for girls and women, not the *exception*. . . .

Intense pressure to conform to cultural ideals is experienced by young girls. Many of them start taking pills, drinking, and smoking in order to control their weight. Others start these behaviors in order to ignore or eradicate feelings or as a reaction to what they must do to cope with growing up female in this culture, where their bodies are up for review every day of their lives.

It is a whole lot easier to believe that the problem is with them, rather than with the culture. It is easier to attack the victim than to try to change the perpetrator, especially when the perpetrator is society. Women who struggle with eating disorders are battling not only their own personal demons but also the demons of their culture. Just as we were taught to tie our shoes and taught to drive a car, we were taught to hate our bodies, our appetites, our needs, and ourselves. We have not been taught to be powerful, rational adults, but instead to be sexy little girls. We have learned how to get along in this culture by following the advice of beauty magazines, diet centers, and other women who are getting face lifts and tummy tucks rather than honoring their age. We have taken the battles raged against women and turned the war against ourselves. Some women respond by staying as numb as possible, with overeating or undereating, alcohol, and drugs. Some live in dark rooms in the despair of depression, and some kill themselves. Whatever method they use, they are trying to stop the pain of living in a culture that doesn't support them, doesn't understand them, and doesn't honor the feminine.

## Not About Food

Eating disorders aren't about food, which is why diets don't work. We have seen over and over that once the reasons for over- or undereating have been understood, processed, and then let go, the behavior stops and the woman's body returns to her natural body size. No dieting, no shots, no weight reduction pills, no deprivation of any kind is necessary. If we stay focused on the symptoms we don't hear the message we are trying to tell ourselves. The very problem that we are trying to get rid of is actually trying to tell us something. When we can finally listen, then our so-called enemies of fat and food can turn into allies. Food and fat are not killing us, the obsession to control them is.

> When I was twelve, my sister got married. It was a huge affair. My part in the wedding was to be one of the bridesmaids. All of her other bridesmaids were older than me, pretty and thin. I was a chubby adolescent with pimples and braces. My mother and sister wanted me to go on a five-hundred-calorie-a-day diet for two months before the wedding. The only way I would do it was if they promised to give me a five-pound bar of Hershey's chocolate the day after the wedding. I lost thirty pounds and everyone said I looked great. But all I could think of was the chocolate I would get the next day. I put the weight back on, plus more, immediately. This was the first of many times I would "yo-yo diet," a practice that left me weighing more than three hundred pounds before I was thirty.
>
> —Maggie

When we hear over and over again that we should be dieting and forcing our bodies to meet an unrealistic standard, we begin to believe that we are at fault. We believe we are weak willed because we are not thin, and failures because we can't keep to the strict deprivation diets we have been told we must follow. Although the prevention and treatment of eating disorders is beginning to change, incorporating the cultural and psychological components, many of us have already had years of experience being misunderstood, mislabeled, and mistreated. . . .

*When I came home from my doctor's appointment I was upset. I didn't know just how upset I was until much later. The doctor had told me for the hundredth time to lose some weight. My cholesterol was up, my blood pressure was dangerously high, and I had back pains all day long.*

*These things worried me and as I sat in the doctor's office I heard myself promising to go on a restrictive diet the very next day. Armed with a book on fat grams, a six-pack of liquid drink mix and some high-fiber bars, I left the doctor's office feeling much better. I was confident that I was back on the road to health and that I would have a much thinner body in just six weeks.*

*However, by the time I got home I was feeling nervous at the thought of a month on the new diet plan. I calmed myself down by telling myself that I could eat anything I wanted tonight because after tonight I would never be "bad" again.*

*By six o'clock I had eaten my dinner. By six-thirty I had eaten a pint of ice cream. By seven o'clock I had made a bowl of popcorn to eat while watching TV. By seven-forty-five I had eaten the popcorn and was starting on the bag of potato chips that I hid from myself in a cabinet above the stove. By eight-thirty I finished the potato chips and had eaten my next day's supply of high-fiber bars. Now I was into some of my liquid diet drinks. By nine-fifteen I was thawing out a frozen cake that was in the freezer. I continued eating throughout the night until twelve o'clock, when I was passed out on the couch in front of the TV, with a raging headache and very painful stomachache. However, the panic I had felt all night long was gone at last.*

*—Lisa*

Lisa was mostly unconscious about what she was doing throughout this whole episode. She only knew that she had to eat, and had to keep on eating until the panic stopped. She had eaten this way many times before and she always felt that she would go on that diet Monday, or on the first of the month, or at least by six weeks before she had to see her doctor again.

Lisa's compulsive eating went on for a very long time and Lisa got more and more depressed and sad, and she put on more and more weight. Her whole world became only what she could or could not eat, how big she was, or how much weight she would lose if she could just stick to a diet. She never got to know what was truly bothering her or making her unhappy. She didn't know why she was depressed; she only knew she was fat. She didn't know why she was sad; she only knew she had no willpower. She didn't know why she was panicky; she only knew that her life was unbearable.

---

## Girls Who Diet Are at Risk of Eating Disorders

Overweight teenagers should exercise rather than diet because even those who diet moderately are at huge risk of developing eating disorders, according to an Australian study.

Girls who go on severe diets are 18 times more likely to develop a disorder such as anorexia, say the researchers.

But those who diet moderately—a much larger number—are five times more at risk of suffering eating problems than the average child.

Two thirds of new cases of eating disorders are in girls who have dieted moderately.

Concerned Counseling, *CCI Journal*, 1998. Available at http://concernedcounseling.com/ccijournal/ed_anorexia_dieting.htm.

---

She had no idea that the real problem was not her eating but the way she was trying to take care of herself. She also didn't know that dieting was actually making her eating disorder worse, and that the cure was not fat-gram information, not liquid diet drinks, not high-fiber bars—not controlling her food whatsoever!

Like Lisa, the compulsive eater eats not only when she is physically hungry, but also when she is emotionally hungry. For the compulsive eater who is a chronic dieter, it's important to stop all diets, to legalize food and let herself eat, becoming her own diet expert and trusting her own body wisdom. This helps the compulsive eater step out of the diet/binge cycle and into her body, relearning the natural cues of physical hunger and fullness. At the same time the compulsive eater can learn how to identify emotional hunger and nurture herself in ways other than food, allowing herself to experience her own feelings without overeating. The compulsive eater also usually feels shame and hatred for her body, but she can work toward loving and accepting her body no matter how different it is from the cultural ideal.

*My girlfriends and I started a diet when we were fifteen years old and were taking gymnastics. We all lost weight, got a lot of attention, and looked good in our leotards. My coach, my peers, and my parents were proud of my athletic abilities and my "look." But, I wanted to get even thinner than that. So I did. I got thinner and thinner until finally the summer of my seventeenth birthday, my parents put me in the hospital. I was force fed and had to go to therapy sessions three times a day. I couldn't stand the weight my body was putting on but I wanted to get out of the hospital as soon as I could. So I gained twenty pounds and they let me go. I felt like I couldn't compete at this "gross weight." I went on another diet and within three months I was down to eighty-five pounds. Again. When I was around my parents, I wore very baggy clothes and pretended to eat by hiding food in my napkin to be thrown away later. Even so, they still watched me like a hawk. Finally I moved out of my parents' house when I was eighteen and was free to eat any way I wanted to. I could not stand not to be "in control" of my body, my food, or my life. I am now twenty-five years old and I've been in the hospital four times. The last time I almost died of a heart attack. I weighed seventy pounds.*

*—Emily*

Girls and women start to starve themselves for many different reasons. Like Emily, some women feel unsafe at their natural weight and feel more secure about themselves the thinner they become. The anorexic gets panicky when she is not in control or not perfect, which manifests in her insistence on maintaining her weight below her natural weight. She experiences an unrelenting and intense fear of gaining weight. Often the anorexic looks into the mirror and instead of seeing an emaciated woman she sees someone who is fat. Her own self-perceptions are distorted and she often has feelings of self-hatred and disgust. When an anorexic first starts dieting, she often gets a lot of positive feedback, from friends, family, and the culture. Sometimes it is only after she has lost 10 to 20 percent of her natural body weight that anyone starts to get worried. This is too late—she is already hooked on the anorexic way of life: fasting, obsessive exercising, control. Her recovery depends on being willing to let go and trust her body and her feelings, love herself as she is, and tap into her own will to live. These are women whose obsessions are killing them.

> *I began dieting at thirteen and started throwing up at sixteen, after I saw another friend do it. At first it was just something I'd do now and then, after I'd eaten too much or when I felt too fat. But soon it seemed like I was eating too much too often and feeling fat all the time. In college I started running to try to keep my weight down, but I couldn't stop eating. The academic and social stress was just too much for me. I remember at night going from vending machine to vending machine, trying to fill this insatiable need to eat, and then feeling so disgusted afterward I would find the nearest bathroom and throw up. Only then would I feel calm enough to sit down and study. Soon it became a way of life for me, and I was throwing up three to four times a day. I lived with hatred and disgust with myself for this behavior, but there was nothing I could do to stop it. I would begin every day by telling myself that I was going on a diet and would stop eating and then wouldn't have to throw up. I would end every day by hating myself for all the food I ate, for all the times I threw up, and for how fat my body was. I was in the middle of a destructive, depressing cycle and couldn't see my way out.*

> *—Laura*

Like Laura, many bulimic women started purging after they had "failed" at dieting. They either felt they were eating too much, or their body was too fat, or both. Laura began purging by throwing up, and then began overexercising as a way to get rid of the food and weight. Other women use laxatives, diuretics, enemas, other medications, or fasting as a way to purge. Purging usually occurs after a binge in which a large amount of food is eaten. However purging can occur anytime and is frequently a response to overwhelming feelings. For the experienced bulimic, just the feeling of even small amounts of food in the stomach can trigger the need to purge. The binge/purge cycle itself can be self-perpetuating because the shame and anger from purging can create the need to soothe oneself with food, creating another binge that once again needs to be purged. Bulimic women, like their sister anorexics and compulsive eaters, usually spend a lot of time being concerned with their food and their weight. And like their sisters, bulimics also tend to have difficulty not only soothing themselves emotionally but containing and processing overwhelming feelings. In recovery, bulimics must learn to sit with the feelings, the fullness, and the weight without purging, and also learn to take care of themselves emotionally without using food.

Lisa's, Emily's, and Laura's stories are not uncommon among women with eating disorders. Eating disorders are heartbreaking and fill people with despair. However there is a cure and it is powerful: to listen to what your eating problem is trying to tell you is the way through to the other side of your disorder. This process is what we call *going beyond hunger*, to achieve freedom from your overeating, the diet/binge cycle, and self-starvation. . . .

Living a life beyond hunger means finding true recovery. Recovery means no more obsession about food and weight. Recovery means knowing who you are and what you want, and being able to communicate those desires. Recovery is knowing that you have a right to be here and take up as much space as you do. You no longer have to make sure your body gets so small as to disappear or to get so big that you are sure to be seen. There *is* an alternative. You can start speaking with your voice instead of your body. Recovery is being proud of the size you are, the age you are, the color you are, the sex you are, and the person you are. Recovery is getting your life back, being your own true self, and living life to its fullest.

# Periodical Bibliography

The following articles have been selected to supplement the diverse views presented in this chapter. Addresses are provided for periodicals not indexed in the *Readers' Guide to Periodical Literature*, the *Alternative Press Index*, the *Social Sciences Index*, or the *Index to Legal Periodicals and Books*.

| | |
|---|---|
| *BBC News* | "TV Brings Eating Disorders to Fiji," May 20, 1999. Available at http://news.bbc.co.uk/hi/english/health/newsid_347000/347637.stm. |
| Amy Beck | "Pornography Ignites the Self-Destructive Pursuit of Perfection," *Harvard Crimson*, March 19, 1998. Available at www.studentadvantage.com/article_story/1,1075,c5-i45-t210-a12822,00.html. |
| *Harvard Mental Health Letter* | "Eating Disorders," October 1997. |
| Merry N. Miller and Andrés Pumariega | "Culture and Eating Disorders," *Psychiatric Times*, February 1999. Available at www.mhsource.com/pt/p990238.html. |
| Eric Stice, Diane Spangler, and W. Stewart Agras | "Ultra-Thin Magazine Models Negatively Impact Girls with Pre-Existing Body Image Dissatisfaction," *Self-Help Magazine*, September 12, 1999. Available at www.shpm.com/articles/eating/magmodels.html. |
| *Well-Connected* | "Eating Disorders: Anorexia and Bulimia," *WebMd/Lycos*. Available at http://webmd.lycos.com/content/dmk/dmk_article_40031. |
| Jill S. Zimmerman | "An Image to Heal," *Humanist*, January/February 1997. |

# CHAPTER 4

# How Should Eating Disorders Be Treated?

# Chapter Preface

Although approximately half of all sufferers of eating disorders eventually achieve recovery, reliable treatment for these disorders has proven elusive. One significant obstacle to treating anorexia is that anorexics often deny that they have a problem. As the writers for *Well-Connected* explain, the anorexic patient "believes that the emaciation is normal and even attractive. . . . Even worse, the anorexic condition may be encouraged by friends who envy thinness."

Because anorexics suffer from an overwhelming fear of gaining weight and therefore simply refuse to eat, many do not recover. This creates the difficult dilemma of whether or not it is ever appropriate for doctors to force-feed an unwilling anorexic. Janice Russell, senior lecturer in the Department of Psychiatry at the University of Sydney, arguing in favor of protecting anorexics' lives at all costs, states that "most [doctors] can recall a patient treated coercively who made a full recovery and later sincerely thanked us for doing what was experienced at the time as totally reprehensible."

On the other hand, Heather Draper, a lecturer in biomedical ethics at the University of Birmingham, contends that clinicians should respect adult anorexics' decision to refuse treatment. She writes, "Perhaps in the context of making decisions about the quality of their lives it is wrong not to allow anorexics the right to refuse therapy. It will be difficult to determine which anorexics can competently judge that they have reached the end of the road. . . . Equally, it will be difficult to watch them die when it is possible to prolong their lives. But these difficulties should not deter us from trying to do our best by all anorexics, not just the majority."

The fact that eating disorder patients often do not wish to be cured makes treatment a difficult and sometimes controversial process. Authors in the following chapter discuss other problems related to the treatment of people with eating disorders and offer different perspectives on how these disorders can be remedied.

> "If eating behavior . . . is simply the result of a mixture of neurotransmitters, then a pharmaceutical intervention may be more effective than attempts at behavior modification."

# Pharmacological Drugs May Help People with Eating Disorders

*Medical Sciences Bulletin*

In the subsequent viewpoint, the *Medical Sciences Bulletin* states that people with low levels of serotonin—a brain chemical that regulates mood—are at risk of developing eating disorders. Consequently, the author argues, drugs that boost levels of serotonin, called selective serotonin-reuptake inhibitors (SSRIs), can successfully treat these disorders. In particular, SSRIs have proven to be effective in reducing the bingeing and vomiting episodes of bulimic patients. The *Medical Sciences Bulletin* is an Internet journal of pharmacology and therapeutics.

As you read, consider the following questions:
1. Why do people with low levels of serotonin overeat, in the author's view?
2. How have anorexics responded to drug therapy, as stated by the *Medical Sciences Bulletin*?
3. What proof does the author offer that bulimic patients respond well to drug treatment?

It is increasingly recognized that obesity is not a failure of will or behavior, nor is it a disorder of body weight regulation. It is a chronic medical condition, like hypertension or diabetes. In the obese person, body weight is just as carefully regulated as it is in nonobese persons, but regulation is around an elevated set point. This homeostatic set point—strongly influenced by genetics and extraordinarily difficult to alter—is probably controlled by neurotransmitters that signal hunger or signal satiety. Only those individuals with exceptional willpower and the ability to tolerate discomfort are able to defeat this homeostatic mechanism through dietary energy restriction. A number of major studies have shown that the majority of dieters who lose weight with low-calorie diets and behavior modification regain that lost weight within 3 to 5 years.

If eating behavior, like mood and personality, is simply the result of a mixture of neurotransmitters, then a pharmaceutical intervention may be more effective than attempts at behavior modification, just as antidepressants are generally more effective for clinical depression than a psychiatrist. At one time, amphetamines were popular prescription drugs for weight control, although one complaint was that as soon as the drug was discontinued, the patient gained back all the lost weight. However, as obesity researcher Robert Weintraub has pointed out, if obesity is a chronic medical condition in the same way that hypertension is a chronic medical condition, then weight gain following drug discontinuation is no different from rising blood pressure after the discontinuation of antihypertensive medications.

## The Link Between Serotonin and Eating Disorders

In the early 1980s, clinical investigators discovered a link between serotonin and eating disorders. The discovery was serendipitous: during clinical trials of the serotonin reuptake-inhibitor fluoxetine, (Prozac/Lilly), one side effect noted was weight loss. Richard and Judith Wurtman (Massachusetts Institute of Technology) had already implicated serotonin in eating disturbances. They theorized that dietary starch is converted to sugar, sugar stimulates the pancreas to release insulin, insulin raises brain levels of the amino acid tryptophan, tryptophan is a precursor of serotonin, and serotonin regulates mood, producing a sense of well-being. Therefore, obese people load up on carbohydrates to elevate mood. In studies with obese women, Wurtman et al. found that a high-carbohydrate snack improved mood. Moreover, premenstrual women and smokers trying to quit also tended to eat more carbohydrates, which seemed to lift mood.

Subsequent studies showed that serotoninergics helped overeaters reduce snacking and lose weight. One agent—dexfenfluramine (made by the French pharmaceutical firm Les Laboratoires Servier)—was particularly effective for cutting food intake. Dexfenfluramine is the active portion of the serotoninergic antiobesity agent fenfluramine (Pondimin/Robins), and may be more effective than the parent molecule with fewer side effects (dry mouth, diarrhea, unsteadiness, and memory problems). In 1982, the Wurtmans acquired the US patent for dexfenfluramine, and 6 years later they co-founded Interneuron Pharmaceuticals Inc. to commercialize the drug. In 1990, Interneuron went public, and in January 1994 the company filed with the FDA to market the drug. . . .

## Using Pharmacological Drugs to Treat Anorexia and Bulimia

Anorexia nervosa and bulimia nervosa are psychiatric syndromes whose underlying pathology has been described as the relentless pursuit of thinness. The two diseases are separate entities, although there is considerable overlap; about 50% of anorectics binge and purge. Both diseases occur primarily in adolescence and young adulthood, they run a long and protracted course, and they interfere with normal development (social maturation, separation from family of origin, and career decisions). Anorexia has been described in the psychiatric literature for more than a century, but bulimia has only been recognized as a clinical entity since 1978. Patients are challenging and difficult to treat. Indeed, it seems that to be effective, any treatment must ultimately produce thinness. In other words, if a bulimic could achieve thinness without having to vomit, then that patient would be "cured" of bulimia. If an anorectic could achieve thinness without

117

having to starve, that patient could be "cured" of starvation.

The typical patient with anorexia nervosa or bulimia nervosa is female, young, single, and of middle-to-upper socioeconomic status and has previously shown a tendency to obesity. Depressive and obsessional symptoms are common, as are a strong family history of affective disorder. Depression is sometimes attributed to the starvation, which can produce the same psychological profile as that seen in mild to moderate major depression. However, true major depression (either before or after the emaciation) is far more prevalent in anorectic patients than in the general population. Although anorexia and bulimia are more often seen in females, both disorders also occur in males. Sharp et al. described the clinical features of 24 men with anorexia nervosa. Bingeing and vomiting were common (50%, the same as in females). Also remarkably common were depressed mood, early wakening, obsessional symptoms, and a family history of affective disorders and alcohol abuse. Age at onset (18.6 years) and at presentation (20.2 years) was older than in females. The men were mostly single and of higher socioeconomic status and had a premorbid tendency towards obesity. Laxative abuse was less frequent in males than has been reported in females, and excessive exercising was more frequent.

---

## Zofran May Break the Binge/Purge Cycle

A drug used to lessen the side effects of chemotherapy for cancer patients seems to help bulimic women reduce—or even stop—their cycle of binge eating and purging. Results of a small study . . . indicate that the anti-nausea drug Zofran can reduce by half the number of binge/purge episodes in bulimic patients. . . .

"Within two days of taking the medicine, the symptoms disappeared—after 12 years," [stated a] 27-year-old woman, who identified herself only as Cheryl. . . ."I did not have a reduction in symptoms; I had complete remission."

Daniel J. DeNoon, *WebMD*, March 2, 2000.

---

Because of the strong association between anorexia/bulimia and affective disorders, a number of psychotropic drugs have been used to treat patients with anorexia and bulimia, including neuroleptics (chlorpromazine), tricyclic antidepressants (amitryptyline, imipramine), monoamine oxidase inhibitors, and serotonin-reuptake inhibitors (fluoxetine, clomipramine). Bulimics are more apt to respond to therapy—both drug therapy and cognitive-behavioral therapy—but anorectics are notoriously difficult to treat. Certain drugs have proved useful for promoting weight gain during the initial treatment of acute anorexia nervosa, but so far no drug has proved effective for long-term weight maintenance, for changing anorectic attitudes, or for preventing relapse.

## Clinical Trials for Bulimia

Since the pursuit of thinness is the primary motivation in patients with anorexia and bulimia, drugs that hold the promise of appetite control have been more enthusiastically accepted by these patients than other drugs. The serotonin-reuptake inhibitors—which suppress craving and promote weight loss—have been the most successful for controlling symptoms of bulimia. The Fluoxetine Bulimia Nervosa Collaborative Study Group treated 387 bulimic women with either 20 mg or 60 mg of fluoxetine or placebo for 8 weeks. Fluoxetine at 60 mg was significantly superior to placebo for reducing binge eating and vomiting. The 20-mg dose significantly reduced vomiting but not bingeing. Improvement was also seen in depression, carbohydrate craving, and pathological eating habits, especially with the higher dosage. Very few patients dropped out of the study because of adverse effects.

Fluvoxamine (Luvox/Solvay Pharmaceutical) is another serotonin-reuptake inhibitor that has proved to be effective for treating bulimia. In a study of 20 bulimic women, fluvoxamine 50–150 mg/day significantly reduced the mean number of binge eating episodes. Body weight also showed a significant decrease. The drug was generally well tolerated, with sleep disturbances reported most often (both somnolence and insomnia). One patient withdrew after 7 weeks because of persistent insomnia. Because it lacks cardiotoxicity, fluvoxamine is safer for bulimic patients whose excessive vomiting often leads to electrolyte disturbances that have a detrimental effect on the heart.

Trazodone (250–600 mg) has also been shown to reduce both bingeing and vomiting episodes, although the drug has apparently been associated with delirium in bulimic patients. Fenfluramine 60 mg was effective for reducing both bingeing and vomiting in a double-blind study of 15 bulimic patients. Surprisingly, the drug also reduced symptoms of depression. Overall, drug therapy is the most successful when used as part of an overall program that includes cognitive-behavioral therapy to modify eating habits (group therapy is often highly effective), and diet and exercise for weight management. Patients must be taught that there are better paths to thinness than vomiting and purging.

*"Psychologists play a vital role in the successful treatment of eating disorders."*

# Psychotherapy May Help People with Eating Disorders

American Psychological Association

The American Psychological Association (APA), a national society of psychologists, asserts in the following viewpoint that psychotherapy is vital to the treatment of eating disorders. Psychologists can help sufferers of eating disorders replace destructive thoughts and behaviors with positive ones, claims the APA, and can aid patients in resolving the psychological issues that instigated the disorder.

As you read, consider the following questions:

1. What is the link between eating disorders and other mental disorders, as claimed by the APA?
2. What are the various roles that psychotherapy plays in helping sufferers of eating disorders, according to the author?
3. As stated by the APA, how effective is treatment for eating disorders?

Excerpted from American Psychological Association, "How Therapy Helps: Eating Disorders—Psychotherapy's Role in Effective Treatment," October 1998, available at http://helping.apa.org/therapy/eating.html. Reprinted with permission from the American Psychological Association.

Research indicates that eating disorders are one of the psychological problems least likely to be treated. But eating disorders often don't go away on their own. And leaving them untreated can have serious consequences. In fact, the National Institute of Mental Health estimates that one in ten anorexia cases ends in death from starvation, suicide or medical complications like heart attacks or kidney failure.

Eating disorders can devastate the body. Physical problems associated with eating disorders include anemia, palpitations, hair and bone loss, tooth decay, esophagitis and the cessation of menstruation. People with binge eating disorder may develop high blood pressure, diabetes and other problems associated with obesity.

Eating disorders are also associated with other mental disorders like depression. Researchers don't yet know whether eating disorders are symptoms of such problems or whether the problems develop because of the isolation, stigma and physiological changes wrought by the eating disorders themselves. What is clear is that people with eating disorders suffer higher rates of other mental disorders—including depression, anxiety disorders and substance abuse—than other people.

## The Role of Psychologists

Psychologists play a vital role in the successful treatment of eating disorders and are integral members of the multidisciplinary team that may be required to provide patient care. As part of this treatment, a physician may be called on to rule out medical illnesses and determine that the patient is not in immediate physical danger. A nutritionist may be asked to help assess and improve nutritional intake.

Once the psychologist has identified important issues that need attention and developed a treatment plan, he or she helps the patient replace destructive thoughts and behaviors with more positive ones. A psychologist and patient might work together to focus on health rather than weight, for example. Or a patient might keep a food diary as a way of becoming more aware of the types of situations that trigger bingeing.

Simply changing patients' thoughts and behaviors is not

enough, however. To ensure lasting improvement, psychologists and patients must work together to explore the psychological issues underlying the eating disorder. Psychotherapy may need to focus on improving patients' personal relationships. And it may involve helping patients get beyond an event or situation that triggered the disorder in the first place. Group therapy also may be helpful.

---

## Cognitive Therapy for Eating Disorders

In cognitive therapy, you teach the patient how to do cognitive restructuring of how she thinks about her life. You teach her the technique and how to do problem solving. Those are her homework assignments, and she comes to each therapy session with these and works these out with your help. What we say to the patient is, "We know you're terrified of giving up this illness, and we don't expect you to believe these techniques will work, but please keep practicing them because eventually you'll be able to feel better, more confident, and more secure when you can use this logical way of controlling your own behavior." Cognitive behavioral therapy is really teaching a patient techniques to control her own behavior. Hilde Bruch laid the foundations for cognitive therapy in her book *Eating Disorders*. She very nicely stated that therapy with these patients must progress slowly and you must take each small event as it comes up and then deal with that in a concrete manner.

Katherine A. Halmi, *JAMA*, June 24, 1998.

---

Some patients, especially those with bulimia, may benefit from medication. It's important to remember, however, that medication should be used in combination with psychotherapy, not as a replacement for it. Patients who are advised to take medication should be aware of possible side effects and the need for close supervision by a physician.

## Does Treatment Really Work?

Yes. Most cases of eating disorder can be treated successfully by appropriately trained health and mental health care professionals. But treatments do not work instantly. For many patients, treatment may need to be long-term.

Incorporating family or marital therapy into patient care

may help prevent relapses by resolving interpersonal issues related to the eating disorder. Therapists can guide family members in understanding the patient's disorder and learning new techniques for coping with problems. Support groups can also help.

Remember: The sooner treatment starts the better. The longer abnormal eating patterns continue, the more deeply ingrained they become and the more difficult they are to treat.

## Prospects for Recovery

Eating disorders can severely impair people's functioning and health. But the prospects for long-term recovery are good for most people who seek help from appropriate professionals. Qualified therapists such as licensed psychologists with experience in this area can help those who suffer from eating disorders regain control of their eating behaviors and their lives.

*"According to the experts, a patient must be re-fed in a monitored environment—usually a specialized hospital setting—until she regains her target weight."*

# Anorexics Need Hospitalization

David France

In the following viewpoint, David France describes the plight of an anorexic whose insurance company refuses to pay for long-term hospitalization. Insurance companies that deny hospital care to patients with severe eating disorders, argues the organization, are in essence consigning these patients to death. Anorexics need hospitalization in order to restore their weight and to halt their obsession with food. France is national affairs editor of *Glamour* magazine.

As you read, consider the following questions:
1. According to France, how do insurance companies justify their refusal to fund hospitalization for anorexics?
2. What evidence does the author provide that managed care denies essential treatment to anorexics?
3. How can anorexics' obsession with food be broken, as explained by the author?

Excerpted from David France, "Anorexics Sentenced to Death," *Glamour*, August 1998. Reprinted with permission from the author.

Tammy Renter is freezing cold. As she picks her way slowly up the sidewalk to her doctor's office in an imposing concrete medical complex along South Euclid Avenue just outside Sioux Falls, South Dakota, one hand pinches shut the neck of her heavy canvas coat. Never mind that the temperature is 71 degrees. Even inside the waiting room, she is so cold she can barely breathe. She hunkers into the corner of a chair, steadies her sunken, pale eyes, and says: "My body just has a mind of its own."

She means this literally. Of the estimated 500,000 Americans, mostly women, who suffer from anorexia nervosa, some 100,000 have it so severely that they risk dying. Tammy is one of the sickest. At 6 feet tall, she weighs 100 pounds. That's 60 pounds under her ideal body weight. Her doctors have hospitalized her five times in an effort to get her to eat. Nevertheless, she is slighter today than she has ever been and looks decades older than her age, which is only 32. She has so little flesh that lying in a bed racks her with pain.

"No bed is soft enough," she explains, fixing her deep eyes in a feeble stare, "when you're lying on your skeleton."

Looking at Tammy, a Citibank employee, it is barely conceivable that she would not eat, but her instincts have betrayed her. Her body is a machine she no longer knows how to operate. A simple meal plunges her into a tunnel of anxiety and compulsive thinking as dense and unreasonable as the darkest forms of insanity. In fact, even though she only eats a few bites a day at best, thoughts of food consume her mind in ways most of us would find bizarre. She calls this anorexic persona The Voice. "There's a war that goes on in my head. Because rationally, I know that I should eat. But if I eat, there is a voice that's more powerful that says I'm really not too thin. I'm not as sick as they say I am." When she glances at her ravaged body in a mirror it brings her a strange measure of comfort. "Part of me thinks I like what I see," she says.

"Don't ask me why I do it; it's just stupid," she allows in a quiet moment of reflection. "But the anxiety is overwhelming." The skinnier she gets, the more her mind betrays her—and the less she thinks she needs help.

"She is desperately sick, and she belongs in a hospital," is how her psychiatrist, William Fuller, M.D., describes Tammy. Her medical doctor, Kenneth Aspaas, M.D., a local clinician with a background in eating disorders, has recently given her a 20 percent chance of dying from her illness unless she gets long-term inpatient care from eating-disorders specialists.

For a patient whose anorexia is much less advanced than Tammy's, that would mean intensive hospitalization for three and one half months on average and years of regimented outpatient treatment, according to Michael Strober, Ph.D., editor of the *International Journal of Eating Disorders* and director of the Eating Disorders Program at the University of California at Los Angeles Neuropsychiatric Institute. Only such extensive therapy offers any hope of breaking the physical and psychological grip of anorexia, Strober says. The cost of this treatment can easily be upward of $150,000.

But that will not happen for Tammy. Her insurance policy, Aetna U.S. Healthcare, won't pay for it. Despite mounting research showing a biological and genetic cause, managed-care companies for the most part still consider anorexia a strictly psychiatric disorder and thus not covered by medical benefits. Tammy is only allowed 30 days per year of inpatient treatment for psychiatric care and she used that up this past January. So at press time, not halfway through 1999, her doctors must wait until she is even more seriously ill. Only when Aetna U.S. Healthcare believes she is at imminent risk of organ failure will they approve more time—but to a medical hospital, not a psychiatric facility, and only for as many days as it takes for the crisis to pass. In this way, her doctors hope to keep her body from giving up before next January, at which time she'll be covered for another 30 days of inpatient psychiatric care. It's pretty much been the same every year since her anorexia first crept up on her in 1989, when she was 22 and moved away from her parents for the first time.

"We're certainly not saying Tammy Renter isn't ill," says Aetna U.S. Healthcare spokesperson Betsy Sell. "The issue here is whether the service is a covered benefit under the plan. Tammy Renter has a limit."

Tammy is hardly alone. "A lot of the people who need

treatment today are not getting it, and the people who are getting treatment are getting inadequate treatment because of their insurance companies," says Vivian Hanson Meehan, president and founder of the National Association of Anorexia Nervosa and Associated Disorders (ANAD), an advocacy group for those with eating disorders as well as their families and their doctors.

## Treatment Denied

In an exclusive survey *Glamour* conducted in conjunction with ANAD, we found that managed care is pulling the feeding tubes out of starving women. A stunning 96.7 percent of the 109 eating-disorders specialists we interviewed told us that insurance caps have put anorexic patients in "life-threatening situations" by denying sufficient specialized hospital care. And 100 percent say the brief hospitalizations most managed-care policies cover have actually caused some of their patients serious relapses—making their illnesses more intractable, just as giving a tuberculosis patient an inadequate course of antibiotics risks making his or her infection resistant to treatment.

The situation is so desperate that fully 18 percent of the doctors in our survey believe a patient from their institution has died as a direct or indirect result of managed-care company cost management. Anorexia is already the most fatal mental-health disorder for women. Of the estimated 100,000 women in the United States sick enough to be hospitalized with severe anorexia, half will eventually die, according to figures from the National Institute of Mental Health and Katherine Halmi, M.D., director of eating disorders at New York Presbyterian Hospital, Weill Cornell Westchester. A number of eating-disorder experts interviewed for this viewpoint explained that anorexia nervosa often begins as simple dieting. But the self-starvation quickly becomes something akin to the elated feelings of an addictive high, and the quest for victims to lose weight becomes all consuming. Because of this, anorexics are likely to isolate themselves from friends and family and adopt unusual eating behaviors or compulsive attachments to certain foods. They come to believe that through severely restricting their food intake, they are gaining control over their lives—although, in fact, quite the opposite is true: Anorexia is a 24-hour-a-day obsession; it leaves little room to worry about anything else.

To break this pattern, according to the experts, a patient must be re-fed in a monitored environment—usually a specialized hospital setting—until she regains her target weight. This process is slow and requires intensive one-on-one interaction with specialists. Gaining more than three or four pounds a week carries the physical risk of heart failure and systemic shock because organs that have been starved cannot keep up with the increased body mass. Recovery is made even more difficult by the fact that patients typically don't want to get better and routinely try to outwit staff by hiding food beneath mattresses or vomiting it up and then drinking gallons of salt water (to retain water and add pounds) or inserting weights into their vaginas before weigh-ins.

## Managed Care Policies Kill Anorexics

• 83.3 percent of respondents report that they've had to reduce the average hospital stay of diagnosed anorexics in the past five years because of managed care. Nearly half say insurance agents mandate premature discharges of their patients "very often"; because of this, 96.7 percent believe anorexia patients around the country are put in life-threatening situations.

• 100 percent say some of their discharged patients are suffering relapses and a startling 18 percent say at least one patient at their institution has died as a direct or indirect consequence of managed-care coverage limits.

• 29.3 percent consider managed-care policies across the board "very harmful" to their patients; fewer than 1 percent called those policies "beneficial." 98.1 percent of eating-disorders experts think legislation will be necessary to rein in managed-care gatekeepers.

David France, "Anorexics Sentenced to Death," *Glamour*, August 1998.

Only once weight is restored to within 95 percent of normal can counseling and medications like Prozac really make a difference, according to published studies. Discharge a patient before that, and she is likely to relapse, perhaps with tragic consequences. In fact, for a patient released from a hospital while her weight is still below 85 percent of normal, her chances of relapsing are a staggering 50 percent, according to new findings by William T. Howard, M.D., a researcher at Johns Hopkins University School of Public Health. Yet insurance companies routinely limit the number of days they cover thus forcing doctors to discharge patients when they weigh, on average, 84 percent of their normal body weight, our survey shows. In the long run, that practice of discharging patients too early is going to result in a much higher death rate, maintains Walter Kaye, M.D., head of the managed-care committee of the Academy for Eating Disorders and a consultant on our national poll. "I think we're going to see a lot more fatalities as a result of managed care."

Insurance companies, however, point a finger of blame at employers, charging that there are a wide variety of plans available and employers tend to pick the cheap and limited ones. Insurance plans "would go out of business if they provided months of extra treatment that they're not paid for," says Pamela Greenberg, the executive director at American Managed Behavioral Healthcare Association, a group that represents the industry. "It's unfortunate."

Meanwhile, the evidence of managed care's terrible impact on anorexics is mounting. During the summer of 1999 Dr. Halmi and her team completed a study of readmittance data for all their anorexic patients over the past 14 years. In 1984, before managed care was dictating discharge criteria, the figure was near zero. In 1998, nearly one in three patients suffered a relapse—a huge increase that Dr. Halmi attributes to heavy-handed cost cutting that limited patient stays. After a recent interview in Dr. Halmi's White Plains, New York, office, one patient broke into tears out in the hall as she was dragged away by her mother because her coverage had run out. That same week, nine other patients were discharged for the same reason.

"The insurance companies believe they should leave," says Dr. Halmi, throwing one hand in the air. "I would say that half of them, in my estimation, are not ready to go at all. They haven't gotten to their target weight, they're not even close to it. Which means these people who are dreadfully afraid of gaining weight, dreadfully afraid of eating, leave the supportive structure of the inpatient unit, go back out to the real world, and they don't have a chance."

## Terrible Treatment Dilemmas

Hearing her name called, Tammy Renter unfolds herself mechanically from the chair, one very visible joint at a time, like a praying mantis positioning herself in the wind. It has been the same every week for the six years she has been coming to see Dr. Aspaas.

She pivots slowly to greet him, and he cups her fragile hand in his. "Are you on your best behavior, Tammy? How's your eating been going?" he asks.

Tammy does not tell the whole truth on this Wednesday morning: that she has not swallowed a bite of food since Monday's lunch, that her refrigerator at home contains only filtered water and the cabinet is empty except for a long-ignored box of oatmeal. Her words come out in a thick sentence. "Not so great," is all she admits.

Still, he can tell from her brittle demeanor that her mental state has gotten worse, and the deterioration scares him. "So what's it going to take, Tammy?" She is silent, unable to formulate a reply. He is clearly frustrated. "I'm going to try to get you in for a week across the street," he says, pointing toward the forbidding facade of Sioux Valley Hospital. "They may let me do it." Dr. Aspaas thinks he can convince Aetna U.S. Healthcare that she is risking death by starvation. Tammy is that sick.

This is not an ideal solution. The medical hospital has no staff trained to treat anorexia. All the nurses can do for her there is bring her food and monitor her tenuous vital signs. In contrast, the psychiatric hospital across town, Sioux Valley Behavioral Health, though not a facility specializing in eating disorders, is at least marginally equipped to treat her disorder.

But Tammy has no chance of getting her insurance company to cover her at Behavioral Health. Lawrence Osborn, M.D., Aetna U.S. Healthcare's medical director for behavioral health, says psychiatric hospital stays are never billed as medical expenses. Clutching her jacket shut with her spidery fingers, Tammy grimaces. "If you want to see what kind of coverage I can get, you can call them yourself," she says.

He agrees, and tells her to be ready to check in on Monday. "Your brain is so fried," he tells her bluntly, "that you really need to be taken away from your life for a while. If all we get is a few days in a hospital bed, well, that's better than nothing."

*"Is it possible that in some cases living with
. . . anorexia can become so burdensome that
the prospect of death seems preferable?"*

# Some Anorexics Should Be Allowed to Refuse Treatment

Heather Draper

Anorexics are often force-fed in order to save their lives and permit them to recover from the emotional and psychological symptoms of their disorder. However, some anorexics repeatedly return to their pattern of self-starvation once their weight is stabilized. In the following viewpoint, Heather Draper, an instructor at the University of Birmingham, argues that the quality of life of some of these anorexics is abysmal, as they have lost hope of recovery and find repeated forced feedings unpleasant. Draper concludes that these patients should be allowed to refuse medical treatment even if death will result.

As you read, consider the following questions:
1. What point does the author make in citing the case of Samantha Kendall?
2. What principle was upheld in the case of *Re C*, as stated by the author?
3. What "parallel case" does Draper cite to support her view that anorexics should be allowed to refuse treatment?

Reprinted from Heather Draper, "Treating Anorexics Without Consent: Some Reservation," *Journal of Medical Ethics*, February 1998. Reprinted with permission from BMJ Publishing Group.

A norexia nervosa is classified as a mental disorder in the International Classification of Diseases (ICD-10), and between 20–30 anorexics die each year in the UK. There is no consensus about what causes the disorder or how it is to be treated. Feeding without consent usually becomes an issue when without further nutrition the anorexic will begin an irreversible decline to death. Once their weight has stabilised and they are released into out-patient care, many will begin to starve themselves again. The natural cycle for the illness is anything from one to eight years. After eight years, the chances of cure begin to diminish rapidly, and it is also thought that ultimate success can also be adversely affected by repeated episodes of forced feeding.

In August 1997, The Mental Health Commission issued guidance on when anorexics can be detained, treated and fed without consent. Although these notes echoed the law as it already stood, the need for such clarification was highlighted in January 1996 by the death of Nikki Hughes. Acting on legal advice, her doctors refused to feed her without her consent, even though she was anorexic. The claim was that Nikki understood what she was doing and had the right to refuse therapy, even though it would result in her death. The Mental Health Commission guidance makes it clear that it would *not* have been illegal to feed Nikki without her consent, providing such feeding was part of a programme of therapy for her anorexia, or necessary to restore her to a condition where other therapies might have been effective.

Although detention, therapy and feeding without consent may be justified in the majority of cases, one can still have reservations which concern a minority of anorexics whose needs cannot be overlooked simply because they are a minority. For instance, in October 1997, Samantha Kendall died after eighteen years of battling with anorexia. Her case made headline news because her twin sister had died three years earlier, also from anorexia. Her family were reported at the time as saying that Samantha wanted to die. Can it be argued that in her case, feeding would simply have *prolonged* her life rather than *saved* it in the interests of a possible cure?

Also in 1997, another anorexic, Kerry, attempted to gain some control over treatment decisions by signing a living will in which she specifically stated that she did not want to be fed, or undergo other measures to prolong her life, if she became incompetent in the future. At the time she made her living will (with legal help) she was receiving therapy and felt optimistic about her recovery. Past experience, however, of being fed without consent (in her case, being literally held down and forced to swallow a high calorie drink) made her determined not to be fed without her consent again. Is it possible that in some cases living with and receiving therapy for anorexia can become so burdensome that the prospect of death seems preferable? Were the terms of Kerry's living will reasonable?

## Prolonging Life vs. Curing Anorexia

In *Riverside Health NHS Trust v Fox*, the judge determined that feeding did constitute treatment for anorexia because other therapies would not be possible until there had been some steady weight gain. The claim that in some cases feeding may only be *prolonging* life, because an anorexic is incurable, is much more controversial.

O'Neill attracted more criticism than support from psychiatrists when he published a case study of an anorexic woman who was referred for palliative care. Offering palliative care to anorexics was considered to be collusion at best, giving up on them at worst. This is an understandable response because many anorexics do recover, some after many years. Anorexia is not a terminal illness in the sense that death is inevitable even if treatment is given. With anorexia it is fair to say that where there is life there is at least the hope of improvement. It is nevertheless possible that some will never get well and that for such patients the misery of feeding and precarious, undesired weight gain will never result in the benefit of being able to look back with gratitude at the actions of carers, parents or partners who refused to give up hope. In such cases, it may be reasonable to draw a distinction between prolonging life and curing anorexia.

There is a difficulty, however, with identifying these cases. With other illnesses, it is accepted that a patient should be the lead partner in deciding when the hope of cure is outweighed by the burdens of the illness and the therapy. But because anorexia is categorised as a mental disorder—a characteristic of which is refusal to eat—and because years of starvation may affect an anorexic's competence to make her own treatment decisions, she is not allowed to call a halt to therapy. And neither are her carers, whose role it is not to give up hope either in the prospect of ultimate cure or in the abilities of the anorexic to find the cure within herself. It is an additional tragedy of anorexia nervosa that the tiny minority of incurable sufferers are trapped by the logic of the definition of the illness and the philosophy of the therapy.

## Refusing Therapy

In the UK, competent individuals have the right to give or refuse their consent to medical intervention. This right can be exercised with or without giving reasons, and irrespective of whether the reasons given are rational. This right also extends to the mentally ill, for the only interventions which can be given without consent are those administered in connection with their mental illness; other interventions are specifically excluded by the Mental Health Act. This was reinforced in common law in *Re C* when the court upheld the refusal of a schizophrenic patient, detained under the act, to have his gangrenous leg amputated. Professional carers are advised that the nature of the decision to be made and the nature of the information required to make it, are vital in determining competence.

Even though anorexia is a mental illness, it is not obvious that anorexics are incompetent to make *any* decisions for themselves. Some are being treated for anorexia whilst at the same time working in responsible jobs, running their own finances etc. They are likely to be totally incompetent only at the point of starvation. The view that anorexics are specifically not competent to make treatment decisions is based on the judgments that they are somehow driven by their anorexia (and their behaviour is, therefore, involuntary) and that they hold irrational views about their body image.

My own—not uncontroversial—view is that it might be possible for anorexics to be incompetent to make treatment decisions but nevertheless competent to make decisions about the quality of their lives as anorexics undergoing therapy. Two different kinds of refusal of consent to therapy may be confused in the assessment of a small minority of anorexics. The first is the refusal to eat, which may be regarded as involuntary and irrational. The second is the decision to refuse all therapy (including food) because the quality of life with anorexia is not good enough to outweigh the burdens of the therapy. Any decision that life is not worth living can be challenged by someone else for whom life in similar circumstances does seem worth having. But whilst we are justified in questioning her decisions, are we right to exclude the anorexic from the decision-making?

## Hospitalization Is No Panacea

Gaining weight while hospitalized is no guarantee of long-term success; anorectic patients are sometimes said to "eat their way out of the hospital" and then stop. Their emotional condition may improve when their weight is closer to normal, but preventing relapse is difficult, partly because of the tendency to deny the illness.

*Harvard Mental Health Letter*, November 1997.

Let us take a step back from the emotionally charged issue of anorexia and consider a parallel case—that of a woman who knows that with a radical mastectomy and chemotherapy she has a good chance of recovering from breast cancer but who refuses to have the surgery because, in her opinion, living with only one breast or no breasts at all will be intolerable. She is *also* making a decision based on her perception of her body image and we might think that this is an irrational perception. Nevertheless, operating without her consent is unthinkable.

Certain cases of anorexia permit a similar verdict. Anorexics who have suffered from the condition beyond the extreme end of the natural cycle are in a strong position to judge what life with anorexia is like and therefore are also in a position to determine whether prolonging treatment is worth the accompanying burdens. A. Crisp's experience of working with anorexics prompted him to write:

(m)any anorexics feel constantly like alcoholics, that they are just one step away from disaster. When suicide occurs, it is often within this context. The individual is seeking relief from the endless terror and exhaustion of a battle to maintain her position.

Perhaps in the context of making decisions about the quality of their lives it is wrong not to allow anorexics the right to refuse therapy. It will be difficult to determine which anorexics can competently judge that they have reached the end of the road so as to protect from themselves the majority who cannot. Equally, it will be difficult to watch them die when it is possible to prolong their lives. But these difficulties should not deter us from trying to do our best by all anorexics, not just the majority.

# Periodical Bibliography

The following articles have been selected to supplement the diverse views presented in this chapter. Addresses are provided for periodicals not indexed in the *Readers' Guide to Periodical Literature*, the *Alternative Press Index*, the *Social Sciences Index*, or the *Index to Legal Periodicals and Books*.

| | |
|---|---|
| *American Family Physician* | "Treatments for Patients with Eating Disorders," October 15, 1999. |
| Heather Draper | "Treating Anorexics Without Consent: Some Reservations," *Journal of Medical Ethics*, February 1998. Available from 2323 Randolph Ave., Avenel, NJ 07001. |
| Mark Stuart Ellison | "Light Therapy May Help Anorexics," *Suite101.com*, May 16, 2000. Available at www.suite101.com/article.cfm/4223/39510. |
| Katherine A. Halmi | "A Twenty-Four-Year-Old Woman with Anorexia Nervosa," *JAMA*, June 24, 1998. |
| *Harvard Mental Health Letter* | "Eating Disorders—Part II," November 1997. |
| Kristin Leutwyler | "Treating Eating Disorders," *Scientific American*, March 2, 1998. |
| Janice Russell | "Treating Anorexia Nervosa," *British Medical Journal*, September 2, 1995. |
| Betsy Streisand | "Overcoming Anorexia," *U.S. News & World Report*, September 29, 1997. |

# CHAPTER 5

# How Can Eating Disorders Be Prevented?

# Chapter Preface

In July 2000, a group of fashion editors, photographers, and feminist activists met in London for the Body Image Summit, a series of speeches and discussions that attempted to address the effects on society of media images of extremely thin women. Many at the conference criticized the fashion industry for promoting a "thin ideal" that most women cannot attain without adopting disordered eating habits.

Prompted by the summit's discussion of the relationship between the media and eating disorders, the British government established a self-regulatory code under which fashion magazines will refuse to feature models that are considered to be unhealthily thin. A few prominent figures in the fashion industry supported the regulations. Liz Jones, editor of *Marie Claire* magazine and a former anorexic, stated, "In the future, if an agency sends us a model whose bones show through her skin, we will send her back. We will also recommend to the agency and to other magazines not to use her."

Other magazine editors argue that the fashion industry is not responsible for eating disorders and in fact encourages women to maintain healthier diets. As Alexandra Shulman, editor of British *Vogue*, states, "We live in a culture that celebrates thinness and I'm not sure we should change that. It is much easier to be fat. If you don't care about yourself, if you eat junk food . . . chances are you will be fat." Shulman also maintains that "anorexia is not a disease caught by handling the pages of *Vogue*," but rather a complex psychological disorder.

So far, neither the U.S. government nor the American media have made any attempt to regulate the images of women portrayed on television, in films, or in magazines. However, many experts believe that curbing such images is an important aspect of preventing women from developing eating disorders. This and other means of eating disorder prevention are discussed in further detail in the subsequent chapter.

"*Eating disorder educational programs . . .
have many benefits for both parents and
teens.*"

# Educational Programs Can Help Prevent Eating Disorders

Joanna Poppink

Joanna Poppink states in the following viewpoint that educational programs are an essential part of society's attempt to prevent eating disorders. She contends that such programs not only deter healthy teenagers from developing an eating disorder, but also encourage those who have symptoms of a disorder to seek help. Poppink, a certified marriage and family therapist, specializes in working with sufferers of eating disorders and with people who are trying to understand and help a loved one who has an eating disorder.

As you read, consider the following questions:

1. Why are parents sometimes afraid that educational materials about eating disorders will cause their children to develop eating disorders, according to the author?
2. In the author's opinion, why do eating disorders usually go undetected in their early stages?
3. How can eating disorder education change parents' attitudes, as explained by the author?

Reprinted from Joanna Poppink, "Eating Disorder Education: Benefits for Parents and Teens," *Self-Help Magazine*, May 28, 1999. Reprinted with permission from the author. To learn more about the author go to www.joannapoppink.com.

Sometimes parents are afraid that educational materials about eating disorders will stimulate an eating disorder in their teenager. They also fear such material will encourage a teenager with an eating disorder to try new and different methods of acting out the illness. Sometimes loving parents are afraid to know specific information about eating disorders themselves. They think that if they ignore the subject it will keep the disorder out of their lives.

While providing information is powerful, I want to reassure parents that information about eating disorders will not cause an eating disorder to develop in their child. By the same token, such information will not cure a person, teen or any age, who is suffering from an eating disorder. Treatment consisting of compassion, understanding, and specific clinical expertise is required for recovery.

## The Benefits of Educational Programs

While eating disorder educational programs will not cure an existing eating disorder, such programs have many benefits for both parents and teens. Programs can:

1. alert parents and children to the nature of eating disorders,
2. show the physical and psychological risks involved in acting out an eating disorder,
3. explain how to recognize when they or someone they know needs help,
4. and most importantly describe many ways to start treatment and bring help and guidance to the individual with the eating disorder and their families.

Educational programs are needed because often early stages of an eating disorder go unrecognized by everyone, including the person with the disorder. Everyone eats. Plus, there are many ways of eating and not eating that are socially sanctioned for particular occasions. For example, it's socially acceptable to eat junk food, even large quantities of it, at parties or at the movies. It's also socially acceptable to diet and try fad diets that might include fasting. It has become acceptable to acknowledge "comfort foods" such as chocolate or ice cream as means of coping with stress or disappointment.

## School-Based Health Education Programs Can Have a Positive Effect

A recent study . . . reported encouraging findings in using a new self-esteem approach for improving body image, eating attitudes, and behaviors among 470 male and female adolescents. The study found significant and lasting improvements in students' body satisfaction and physical self-concept as well as reductions in the importance of peer group acceptability, physical appearance, and athletic competence. Dieting and weight loss were prevented among females. Among students considered at greatest risk for eating disorders . . . similar improvements were established and generally maintained during a 12-month follow up. Results demonstrated that school-based health education programs, when properly planned and evaluated, can have a positive and lasting impact on body image, eating behaviors, attitudes, and self-image of adolescents.

Jennifer O'Dea and Danielle Maloney, *Journal of School Health*, January 2000.

---

It would be very difficult to distinguish a newly forming bulimic from a non–bulimic person when both are devouring lots of sweets and treats at a pajama party. It would be difficult to distinguish a newly forming anorexic teenager from her teenage friends when they are all experimenting with exotic diets and judging every aspect of their body as too fat. Plus, the anorexic/bulimic who is first experimenting with vomiting, rather than being worried or frightened, is usually quite happy at discovering a "trick" to help her think she is avoiding the consequences of holding and digesting any food she eats. She doesn't know herself that she has found a dangerous activity that helps her dull her ability to feel, to be aware of her surroundings and to respond in a healthy way to stress in her life.

## Stopping Eating Disorders at an Early Stage

Parents may be reassured to know that eating disorder education might be a wake-up call that jars the consciousness of young people in an early stage of an eating disorder. Through education a young girl might recognize herself as being on her way to having a serious disorder.

If she knows the symptoms, knows there is supportive and

caring help available and knows how to ask for that support and help she has an opportunity to get some early healing. With encouragement and support from adults and peers in her environment she has a chance of redirecting herself before the disorder advances to relationship destroying and life destroying levels.

Eating disorder education can help parents become less fearful and more understanding if their child does have an eating disorder. Parents can be empowered to lovingly and more confidently support the healing efforts required for their child to recover. With education and informed family support, the child may be more willing and capable of doing the necessary healing work.

Early education presented clearly and sensitively with regard to the developmental stage of the audience may provide a powerful way of waylaying an eating disorder, encouraging informed and useful family cooperation to help a child grow up healthy and free.

For Educational Resources Contact:

Academy of Eating Disorders (AED)
6728 Old McLean Village Drive
McLean, VA 22101
http://www.acadeatdis.org
(703) 556-9222

American Anorexia and Bulimia Association (AABA)
165 West 46th Street, Suite 1108
New York, NY 10036
http://www.aabainc.org
(212) 575-6200

Anorexia Nervosa and Related Eating Disorders (ANRED)
http://www.anred.com/toc.html
(800) 931-2237

Eating Disorders Awareness and Prevention, Inc. (EDAP)
603 Steward Street, Suite 803
Seattle, WA 98101
http://www.edap.org
(206) 382-3587

International Association of Eating Disorders Professionals
427 Whooping Loop, Suite 1819
Altamonte Springs, FL 32701
http://www.iaedp.com/
(407) 831-7099

> "One-shot [educational] presentations by recovered patients did not help [prevent eating disorders] and might be detrimental."

# Educational Programs May Increase the Incidence of Eating Disorders

Denise Grady

In the subsequent viewpoint, *New York Times* writer Denise Grady presents evidence that educational programs intended to discourage people from developing eating disorders may have the opposite effect. According to Grady, one study demonstrated that a program at Stanford University—similar to those offered at many colleges and universities—may have actually increased the rate of abnormal eating behaviors among participants. Presentations made by thin, attractive women who have experienced eating disorders can be hazardous, the author writes, because listeners may seek to emulate these women's behavior.

As you read, consider the following questions:
1. What two things struck Dr. Mann as she watched the Stanford University presentation on eating disorders, as described by the author?
2. As stated by Grady, what explanations does Dr. Mann offer for why the Stanford program failed?
3. What message about eating disorders should be sent to women who already have symptoms of a disorder, according to Dr. Mann and explained by the author?

Reprinted from Denise Grady, "Efforts to Fight Eating Disorders May Backfire," *The New York Times*, May 7, 1997. Reprinted with permission from *The New York Times*.

What better way to prevent eating disorders among young women in college than to let them hear first-hand the harrowing tales of others who have had those conditions? It is an approach used on many campuses in this country.

But one such program, designed by students at Stanford University, turned out to be a case of good intentions gone awry, researchers have found. It did not prevent eating disorders, and may have even made them worse. Because the program was similar to those offered at many colleges and universities, the researchers have recommended that all those plans be evaluated to determine whether they should be continued.

Eating disorders have become more common in the United States and other developed countries in the last 30 years. Ten percent of American college students are affected, more than 90 percent of them women. The reason for the increase is not known, though social pressures to be thin are assumed to play a role. The disorders are most likely to follow efforts to diet, and teen-age girls who are slightly overweight have the highest risk.

Some become binge eaters, wolfing down huge amounts of food and becoming overweight. Others develop bulimia, bingeing and then "purging" with laxatives, vomiting or other drastic actions to lose weight. Those with a rarer disorder, anorexia nervosa, shun food in a compulsive drive to lose weight, becoming emaciated but nonetheless thinking they look fat. Treatment for anorexia, consisting of psychotherapy and sometimes antidepressant drugs, works for only about a quarter of patients. In 10 percent to 18 percent of cases, the disorder is fatal.

## An Analysis of the Stanford Program

The analysis of the program at Stanford, published in the May issue of the journal *Health Psychology*, began in 1993 when Dr. Traci Mann, the lead author of the study, observed two undergraduates making a presentation about eating disorders to a psychology class. The two young women, one recovered from anorexia and the other from bulimia, were members of a student group called Body Image, Food and

Self-Esteem. The group was independent of the university administration, which offered counseling and treatment for eating disorders, but no prevention programs. The students provided objective information about eating disorders and also talked about their own experiences.

As Dr. Mann watched, several things struck her. The two students were slim, attractive, poised and healthy looking, the kind of young women that others might admire and even try to emulate. It also seemed to Dr. Mann that the reality of eating disorders was harsher than these students let on.

"My college roommate had been bulimic," Dr. Mann recalled, "and the most salient thing to me was that she was suffering. She suffered all the time."

## Making Eating Disorders Look "Too Easy"

But Dr. Mann did not think the Stanford students communicated that, or made it clear that people with eating disorders had lost control. "They made it look too easy, as if you could get anorexia, get over it and then be thin and a leader like them," she said. "The presentation separated the behavior from its mental illness aspect."

Dr. Mann decided to study the program. She had 597 female students fill out a questionnaire about their eating and dieting habits and behaviors related to eating disorders. Next, she divided the group and randomly invited only half to hear the students' 90-minute presentation. Then, four and twelve weeks later, she asked both those who had heard the presentation and those who had not to answer the survey again.

On the first questionnaire, 20 percent of the students reported binge-eating, and 21 percent reported fasting. Three percent had induced vomiting to lose weight, and 2 percent had used laxatives. When she compared the responses on the later questionnaires of those who had attended the presentation with those who had not, she found that hearing the information did not lower the rate of abnormal behaviors. In fact, it was associated with a small increase in some of them in the second questionnaire, which then disappeared by the third one.

Dr. Mann offered several explanations for the failure of the program. First, the attractiveness of the speakers might have sent out a different message from the one they were trying to present. "Some people might want to be like them for the wrong reason," she said.

## The Importance of Sending the Right Message

In addition, because the presentation was directed to both healthy women and those who already had eating disorders, it might have reached neither. The messages for those two groups should be different, Dr. Mann said. For instance, healthy women should be warned that eating disorders are chronic and hard to treat and are considered a form of mental illness. But women who already have symptoms may feel so stigmatized by such dire pronouncements that they might avoid treatment. They may be more likely to seek help if the disorders are described less harshly.

---

### Eating Disorder Horror Stories Can Encourage Illness

Eating disorders, in all of their dramatic, stomach-turning detail, have been completely outed. Talk shows are populated with former anorexics and bulimics; magazines routinely run cautionary tales; books, like the recent *Wasted: A Memoir of Anorexia and Bulimia*, offer up every moment of agony; actresses, gymnasts, ballerinas, even princesses come clean. Photos are mandatory—before: skeletal and drawn; after: slender, glowing, articulate, often surrounded by family and boyfriend.

This wellspring of publicity jibes with current American mythology: Secrets are always bad; information—and education—is power; to demystify something is to overcome it. But an odd and dangerous glitch occurs when this philosophy is applied to eating disorders: All the attention tends not only to demystify but to normalize anorexia and bulimia—even, ultimately, to romanticize them.

Michelle Stacey, *Elle*, May 1998.

---

Dr. Katherine Halmi, director of the Eating Disorders Program at Cornell Medical Center in White Plains, N.Y., said Dr. Mann's findings matched those of other researchers. "The evidence is there that merely going into classrooms and having groups and giving information and having recovered people come and talk is not going to be effective," she said. "We ought to stop pouring money into it. We need to think of other strategies."

Dr. C. Barr Taylor, a professor of psychiatry at Stanford who was not involved with Dr. Mann's study, has also studied programs aimed at preventing eating disorders in college students as well as sixth- and seventh-grade girls. Although he questioned Dr. Mann's conclusion that her data showed a harmful effect from the program, he agreed that one-shot presentations by recovered patients did not help and might be detrimental.

"The kids may identify with those peers in exactly the way you don't want," Dr. Taylor said. But he added that long-term education programs could help by changing girls' attitudes about weight. The benefits, though, are not large, he cautioned.

"We have not solved the problem of preventing eating disorders," Dr. Taylor said.

*"What can we implement on a national policy level? First, promote healthy eating, healthy living, and respect for a wide range of body sizes and shapes."*

# The Government Can Help Prevent Eating Disorders

Lisa Berzins

*Editor's Note: The following viewpoint is excerpted from Lisa Berzins' testimony to Congress.*

Society's worship of thinness and prejudice against obesity is responsible for the prevalence of dysfunctional eating, "yo-yo" dieting, and low self-esteem among American women, maintains clinical psychologist Lisa Berzins in the subsequent viewpoint. The government can help change people's attitudes about weight, she argues, by countering negative stereotypes about fatness, contesting the widespread belief that heavy people cannot be healthy, and challenging false claims made by the diet industry.

As you read, consider the following questions:

1. How do overweight and normal weight preschool children describe obese silhouettes, as stated by Berzins?
2. What evidence does the author provide that overweight cannot be cured by dieting?
3. As explained by the author, what steps has the state of Connecticut taken to protect consumers from the diet industry?

Reprinted from Lisa Berzins, "Dying to Be Thin: The Prevention of Eating Disorders and the Role of Federal Policy," Congressional Briefing, 2000.

We must go beyond struggling to treat and prevent eating disorders to look at our cultural preoccupation with thinness and dieting. Our worship of thinness has made low self-esteem and poor body image . . . an expectable aspect of female development. Girls and women often quip in a self-deprecating manner about the inviting prospect of catching anorexia. As of yet, I have not heard of comparable desires to become schizophrenic or depressed or develop any other psychiatric disorder. Contemporary women view their bodies more negatively than at any other time in history and are more likely than not to believe they are fat, even when they are underweight. For men, self-esteem is usually associated with achievement. As Dr. Striegel Moore said, for women, worth is often measured in terms of physical attractiveness and thinness. It is no coincidence, then, that prior to the onset of puberty there are no difference between depression rates between boys and girls, by age 15, girls are twice as likely to become depressed and 10 times as likely to develop an eating disorder than their male peers.

## Prejudice Against Overweight People

Young girls have indicated in surveys that they are more afraid of becoming fat than they are of cancer, nuclear war, or losing their parents. Surveys also report that as many as 30 or 40% of 9-year-old girls and 80% of 10- and 11-year-old girls have dieted. The prejudice against our heavy citizens , which is known as sizeism, runs deep. . . . Disdain towards fat begins early in life. Both normal weight and overweight preschool children describe obese silhouettes as stupid, dirty, lazy, sloppy, mean, and ugly. When presented with a choice between a friend who is handicapped, disfigured, or fat, the vast majority of children as young as 3 and 4 shun the fat child. Sadly, fat children do not differ from their peers in this regard. In one study, a boy who was fat himself, when asked why he chose the fat child last, he said, "Because he looks just like me."

Research has shown that obese individuals are denied educational opportunities, jobs, promotions and housing because of their weight. Americans spend billions in their quest for weight loss only to discover that the only thing that has shrunk is their bank account. The diet industry preys on the desperation and false hope of dieters so as to make hefty profits. 95% of dieters fail to maintain weight loss, but this failure is ironically blamed on the dieters themselves. And in the meantime, despite the proliferation of dieting aids and low-calorie food products, American obesity rates are increasing steadily. In a recent study that I conducted of 54 large sized women, the median immediate weight loss for those enrolled in diet programs was 75 lbs. But after one year, the median amount maintained was 0. The average amount spent was $7,700 with a range of $0 to $50,000. Virtually all participants weighed more than prior to starting their first diet. Weight loss methods included . . . surgery to close off part of the stomach, wiring shut the jaw to prevent eating, and injection of female horse urine . . . 88% of the participants suffered taunts from peers and family members and many reported unsatisfactory experiences with health care professionals. One woman who suffered the loss of her baby was told that it was because she was too fat. Another was told that she would have to live with the pain of an ovarian cyst because she was too fat to operate on. One year later, a more sympathetic doctor removed the grapefruit-sized cyst. Many shared the experience of being admonished to lose weight when seeking help for headaches, colds, and sore throats. It is an unfortunate fact that heavy women often incur health risks by avoiding the humiliation they associate with seeking medical help.

## The Myth About Dieting

The myth is that overweight can be cured by dieting. The truth is that treating overweight by dieting most commonly results in eventual weight gain. Bodies cannot be shaped at will. Weight is a complex result of heredity, culture, and lifestyle. It is not cured by a pill or a product. Some large-sized people maintain a healthy lifestyle yet remain at above-average weight. It is quite possible to be both fit and heavy despite popular beliefs to the contrary. The health risks of being fat have been oversold whereas, the consequences of dieting have been minimized. Not only has yo-yo dieting been associated with higher mortality rates than maintaining an above average but stable weight, recent studies indicate that dieting and weight loss itself can increase the risk of death.

Dieting is clearly a risk factor for the development of an eating disorder among those who are more vulnerable, and is associated with dysfunctional eating patterns, either undereating or overeating, preoccupation with shape, weight, and food, increased irritability, and risk for depression. For predisposed individuals, dieting may contribute to obesity by altering metabolism. Without a comprehensive health promotion . . . the public is often faced with confusing or contradictory information. Experts concerned with the prevention of eating disorders decry the excessive emphasis on dieting, an obsession with an unattainable ideal of thinness. Those who focus on the treatment of obesity warn of the dangers of excess weight and point to poor eating habits, a high-fat diet, and lack of exercise. Such polarizing positions are divisive and myopic. They do little more than blame either society or the individual. It is time to shift the focus from weight to wellness with a positive emphasis on maximizing health for people of all sizes.

## How the Government Can Help

What can we implement on a national policy level? First, promote healthy eating, healthy living, and respect for a wide range of body sizes and shapes in contrast to rigid meal plans, prescriptive exercise routines, and an emphasis on slenderness. Focus on the benefits of health-enhancing behaviors with the recognition that bodies cannot be shaped at will. For example, Canada has an innovative Vitality approach which provides an excellent model. Both as a concept and a program, it was launched with a national public awareness campaign with the slogan, "Enjoy eating well, being active, and feeling good about yourself." Vitality's focus on health instead of weight advocates stopping the obsession with weight, being healthy with the weight one happens to have, and getting on with life. P.L.E.A.S.E, the organization that I founded, is now also called Vitality Wellness for All Shapes and Sizes and there's information describing it; it's very similar in its approach.

Finally, challenge sizeism. Emphasize a respect for a variety of sizes and shapes and the concept of diversity. Increased tolerance and reduced stigmatization, bullying and teasing, beginning in elementary school. A unique approach that I have used with audiences of all ages involves my wearing a padded suit which makes me look twice my size. After I shed it during an intermission during my presentation, people have been able to voice their prejudicial attitudes toward me that were based on my supposedly large-sized appearance. People confessed that they disregarded my arguments until I shed my clothes and became thin. I call it challenging fattitudes.

Reprinted with permission from Kirk Anderson.

Third, increase media literacy. Girls who strongly identify with and who wish to emulate the ideal portrayed in the mass media are most vulnerable to developing eating disorders, poor body image, and low self-esteem. Becoming a savvy consumer and differentiating self from image, can be fostered by efforts to emphasize that advertisers in the dieting and cosmetics industry target and create insecurities about appearance so as to sell their products. Also, encourage families to provide support for their childrens' healthy growth and development. Provide education and reassurance about diversity of size and shape and the importance of challenging media messages that glorify thinness and equate appearance with self-worth.

The Girl Power campaign that was launched by the Department of Health and Human Services fosters self-esteem and self-confidence in girls by encouraging them to pursue their interests while providing skill-building opportunities in mathematics, science, and other academics, athletics, and the arts. Encourage diverse, realistic, and representative role models.

## The Need for Consumer Protections

In terms of health care and consumer protections, one, increase regulation of advertising that targets children as consumers for weight loss products, cosmetics, and apparel. I'm very proud to say that we have succeeded in Connecticut. Connecticut is the first state in the country to enact legislation that requires the diet industry to disclose accurate information regarding average amounts of weight loss maintained based on scientific data that's drawn from representative samples from customers that use their products. And if they don't do that, they have to have a statement that for many dieters, weight loss is temporary. We had a signing ceremony for a second law requiring full disclosure of cost, estimated duration of services, the credentials of program staff, and a 3-day cancellation period without liability. . . . We would very much like to see this happen on a federal level. The Center for Science in the Public Interest which is based in Washington has petitioned the FCC to adopt similar rulings. . . . We really need Congress to put pressure on the FCC about that.

Ensure that prescription weight loss drugs such as Phen-Fen are prescribed as directed and not exploited for cosmetic or economic reasons. Monitor the weight loss industry and hold it responsible for its results in the same way that other health care providers and health care products must be accountable. Include eating disorders awareness in the Healthy People 2000 campaign. This campaign focuses on increasing physical fitness in association with weight control. The campaign needs to highlight the risks associated with dieting and prevention of eating disorders. Eating disorders are mentioned nowhere in the campaign. Finally, reduce size prejudice in health care. Eliminate the use of the traditional height-weight tables; they are based on averages in the general population and have little bearing on individuals than would be determining the desired height based on given weight. Many large women avoid seeking health care because of the treatment they often receive. Require integrated training for providers on eating disorders, nutrition, and obesity. And finally, in terms of research, study the relationship between weight loss and gain, dieting and yo-yo dieting to physical and psychological health, especially self-esteem, and determine which overweight persons have risks factors enough to warrant dieting.

*"Parents can do a lot to prevent eating disorders in early adolescence."*

# Parents Can Help Prevent Eating Disorders

Susan Spaeth Cherry

Susan Spaeth Cherry, a freelance writer and mother of two daughters, proposes in the following viewpoint that parents play an important part in preventing eating disorders. She claims that parents can help ease the anxieties of adolescence by explaining to their children that it is normal for their weight to increase as their bodies grow. Other steps parents can take to prevent their children from developing an eating disorder are to refrain from commenting on people's figures, avoid buying magazines that feature extremely thin models, and keep fresh, healthy food available at all times. Parents can also help prevent eating disorders by fostering high self-esteem in their children, Cherry claims.

As you read, consider the following questions:
1. What reasons does Cherry offer for why eating disorders begin in early adolescence?
2. How can parents make food a "non-issue," in the author's opinion?
3. As explained by the author, how is self-esteem linked to eating disorders?

Reprinted from Susan Spaeth Cherry, "Eating Disorders in Young Teens: Building Self-Esteem Will Help Your Teen Fight These Disorders," 1997, available at family.com. Reprinted with permission from the author.

Most 10 through 14-year-olds are insecure about their bodies, which undergo rapid changes during puberty. Fueled by an intense desire to be like their peers, early adolescents spend a lot of time worrying about their height and weight and the size of their noses, feet, genitals. In a national survey of 8,000 fifth to ninth graders, only 45 percent of girls and 59 percent of boys responded, "often true" or "very often true" to the statement, "I feel good about my body."

This insecurity makes young teens vulnerable to developing eating disorders, such as anorexia nervosa, an intense fear of gaining weight that can lead to endless dieting and even starvation; and bulimia, binge eating followed by purging through laxatives and vomiting. Girls tend to have eating disorders more often than boys.

Eighty-six percent of those with eating disturbances develop food-related problems by their 20th birthdays, according to the National Association of Anorexia Nervosa and Associated Disorders. Of these, 10 percent say their problems started at age 10 or younger, and 33 percent say they began at ages 11 to 15.

## Why Eating Disorders Begin in Early Adolescence

There are several reasons eating disorders begin in early adolescence. Many young teens want desperately to gain mastery over their bodies, which often seem out of control. An early adolescent might say to herself, "I can't grow tall enough to make the basketball team or change the size of my ears, but I can affect my weight through my eating!"

In addition, young teens, who are usually susceptible to media influence, tend to use slender celebrities as role models for how they themselves should look. Movies, TV shows, music videos, magazine articles and ads for health clubs and weight loss programs perpetuate appearance standards that adolescents adopt, but may not be able to meet. Some young teens, especially girls whose mothers diet constantly and complain about their own weight, develop eating disorders because they feel their parents value thinness. In a Yale University study, 82 percent of seventh and eighth graders said they think adults place high value on the idea that "a girl diets to stay thin."

Early adolescent girls can develop eating disorders because of involvement with gymnastics, ballet, or sports where thin, child-like bodies are considered advantageous. "Some coaches require girls to lose so much body fat that they stop having their periods," says early adolescence expert, Cynthia Mee, assistant professor at National-Louis University in Evanston, IL.

Young teens sometimes diet excessively to ward off puberty, a time of complicated sexual feelings and uncomfortable encounters with the opposite sex. Many become obsessed with weight to avoid focusing on other stresses in their lives, such as troubles at home or school.

## What Parents Can Do

Parents can do a lot to prevent eating disorders in early adolescence, experts say. Begin by telling your child what body changes to expect during the early teen years. "Kids have to understand that as their bodies are growing, muscle mass is growing, too. They're also developing more bone, so, of course, their weight is going to increase. But this is not a problem," says Mee.

Avoid commenting on other people's figures, especially your own and your teen's. Don't recommend that your adolescent wear certain clothes to look thinner and try to be positive about her changing body, even if you get negative feedback.

---

### The Importance of Modeling Healthy Eating

Many girls who develop eating disorders have mothers or fathers who diet rigorously. Many put their daughters on diets while they're still in elementary school. One clear fact about eating disorders: Dieting is a risk factor. The more a person diets, the more likely it is that she will develop a disorder.

Stefanie Gilbert, *Washington Post*, April 13, 1999.

---

"Middle schoolers are mentally criticizing their own looks constantly, even when they act arrogant and vain. As a result, even neutral or well-intentioned, positive remarks may be misinterpreted," warns Judith Baenenm author of two National Middle School Association pamphlets on early adolescence.

Avoid buying magazines that glorify thinness, and point

out unrealistic media portrayals of the "ideal" body, whether female or male. Boys can benefit from this practice as much as girls.

Make food a "non-issue," recommends Ann Caron, author of *Don't Stop Loving Me: A Reassuring Guide for Mothers of Adolescent Daughters*. Parents "should keep fresh, healthful food readily available in the house, serve well-balanced meals, and then forget about what the girls eat outside of the house," says Caron. "No one has died from eating junk food, but girls have died from self-inflicted starvation."

## Fostering High Self-Esteem

Foster high self-esteem by showing interest in your early adolescent's feelings, interests, and abilities. Young teens who feel worthless may starve themselves due to an unconscious desire to "disappear" or to alarm parents into providing more nurturing. They may also overeat to fill emotional emptiness and purge later, a symbolic way of spitting out negative feelings they haven't been allowed to express.

Emphasizing that your young teen doesn't have to be perfect will help her accept her body, regardless of how it looks. "Let her be who she is, not who you want her to be," advises Mee.

To further prevent eating disorders, don't emphasize the negative aspects of growing up, such as having to work for a living and do endless household chores. If you persuade your early adolescent that it is undesirable to be an adult, she may avoid eating to postpone maturation and remain child-like.

Robin Goldstein, co-author of *Stop Treating Me Like a Kid*, offers this advice for parents of young teens: "If your child is 10 or 11 and talks about being too heavy, keep a watchful eye on her. If she's older, take her repeated complaints or changes in eating habits seriously."

It's better to deal with the issue now, because the older she gets, the harder it may be to help her accept herself. If you are really worried, you might want to talk to a counselor. A professional can often prevent serious eating problems and help your child view herself more realistically.

# Periodical Bibliography

The following articles have been selected to supplement the diverse views presented in this chapter. Addresses are provided for periodicals not indexed in the *Readers' Guide to Periodical Literature*, the *Alternative Press Index*, the *Social Sciences Index*, or the *Index to Legal Periodicals and Books*.

| | |
|---|---|
| Peggy Claude-Pierre | "Anorexia: A Tale of Two Daughters," *Vogue*, September 1997. |
| Rebecca C. Cohen and Tobin Levy | "Overcoming an Eating Disorder: A Mother-Daughter Journal," *American Health for Women*, October 1997. |
| Stefanie Gilbert | "Parents Can Play a Role in Keeping Eating Disorders at Bay," *Washington Post*, April 13, 1999. |
| *Glamour* | "Stop the Anorexia Obsession," February 1999. |
| Denise Grady | "Efforts to Fight Eating Disorders May Backfire," *The New York Times*, May 7, 1997. |
| Jennifer O'Dea and Danielle Maloney | "Preventing Eating and Body Image Problems in Children and Adolescents Using the Health Promoting Schools Framework," *Journal of School Health*, January 2000. Available from PO Box 708, Kent, OH 44240. |
| Anne Broccolo Philbin | "An Obsession with Being Painfully Thin," *Current Health 2*, January 1996. |
| Betsy Streisand | "Overcoming Anorexia," *U.S. News & World Report*, September 29, 1997. |

# For Further Discussion

## Chapter 1

1. Explain how Brooke C. Wheeler and Donald DeMarco use statistics to support their claims about the prevalence of eating disorders. Whose use of statistics is more convincing, and why?

2. Do you agree with Georgie Binks that eating disorders are not always destructive? Why or why not? How does the list of eating disorders' long-term health effects provided by Sarah Klein influence your view?

3. Do you believe that eating disorders are a serious problem, based on what you have read in this chapter? Why or why not?

## Chapter 2

1. List the reasons why each of the groups discussed in this chapter—adolescent girls, preteens, adult women, female athletes, and men—are at risk of eating disorders. Which author provides the most convincing case? Why?

2. Daryn Eller contends that preteens are more at risk of eating disorders than they were in the past. Suzanne Koudsi makes a similar argument about men. What do their assertions imply about the causes of eating disorders?

3. Based on your reading of the viewpoints in this chapter, which population is most at risk of developing eating disorders? Support your answer with evidence from the viewpoints.

## Chapter 3

1. Ellen Goodman argues that media images of thin women are a partial cause of eating disorders. John Casey disagrees. What reasons do Goodman and Casey provide to support their views? Whose reasoning is more effective, and why?

2. Describe how each of the viewpoints in this chapter uses statistics. Which viewpoint uses statistics most effectively, in your opinion? Why?

3. Consider the various causes of eating disorders proposed in this chapter. Which cause do you find most compelling? Give reasons for your answer.

## Chapter 4

1. Based on what you have read in the viewpoints by David France and Heather Draper, do you think anorexics need to be hospitalized? Provide support for your claim.

2. How do the *Medical Sciences Bulletin* and the American Psycho-

logical Association differ in their approach to treating eating disorders? How do their contrasting views of the causes of eating disorders influence their differing approaches to treatment?

## Chapter 5

1. According to Joanna Poppink, what are the benefits of educational programs intended to prevent eating disorders? What are the risks of such programs, as outlined by Denise Grady? In your opinion, do the risks of educational programs outweigh the benefits, or vice versa? Give reasons to support your answer.

2. Based on your study of the viewpoints by Lisa Berzins and Susan Spaeth Cherry, who plays the most crucial role in preventing eating disorders: the government or parents? Explain your answer.

3. In your view, which of the prevention methods discussed in this chapter is the most promising means of deterring young people from developing eating disorders? Why?

# Organizations to Contact

The editors have compiled the following list of organizations concerned with the issues debated in this book. The descriptions are derived from materials provided by the organizations. All have publications or information available for interested readers. The list was compiled on the date of publication of the present volume; the information provided here may change. Be aware that many organizations take several weeks or longer to respond to inquiries, so allow as much time as possible.

**American Anorexia/Bulimia Association, Inc. (AA/BA)**
165 W. 46th St., #1108, New York, NY 10036
(212) 575-6200
e-mail: amanbu@aol.com
website: http://members.aol.com/amanbu

AA/BA is a nonprofit organization that works to prevent eating disorders by informing the public about their prevalence, early warning signs, and symptoms. AA/BA also provides information about effective treatments to sufferers and their families and friends.

**American Psychiatric Association (APA)**
1400 K St. NW, Washington, DC 20005
(202) 682-6000 • fax: (202) 682-6850
e-mail: apa@psych.org • website: www.psych.org

APA is an organization of psychiatrists dedicated to studying the nature, treatment, and prevention of mental disorders. It helps create mental health policies, distributes information about psychiatry, and promotes psychiatric research and education. APA publishes the monthly *American Journal of Psychiatry*.

**American Psychological Association**
750 First St. NE, Washington, DC 20002-4242
(202) 336-5500 • fax: (202) 336-5708
e-mail: public.affairs@apa.org • website: www.apa.org

This society of psychologists aims to "advance psychology as a science, as a profession, and as a means of promoting human welfare." It produces numerous publications, including the monthly journal *American Psychologist*, the monthly newspaper *APA Monitor*, and the quarterly *Journal of Abnormal Psychology*.

**Anorexia Nervosa and Bulimia Association (ANAB)**
767 Bayridge Dr., PO Box 20058
Kingston, ON K7P 1C0 Canada
website: www.ams.queensu.ca/anab/

ANAB is a nonprofit organization made up of health professionals, volunteers, and past and present victims of eating disorders and their families and friends. The organization advocates and coordinates support for individuals affected directly or indirectly by eating disorders. As part of its effort to offer a broad range of current information, opinion, and/or advice concerning eating disorders, body image, and related issues, ANAB produces the quarterly newsletter *Reflections*.

**Anorexia Nervosa and Related Eating Disorders, Inc. (ANRED)**
PO Box 5102, Eugene, OR 97405
(503) 344-1144
website: www.anred.com

ANRED is a nonprofit organization that provides information about anorexia nervosa, bulimia nervosa, binge eating disorder, compulsive exercising, and other lesser-known food and weight disorders, including details about recovery and prevention. ANRED offers workshops, individual and professional training, as well as local community education. It also produces a monthly newsletter.

**Eating Disorders Awareness and Prevention, Inc. (EDAP)**
603 Stewart St., Suite 803, Seattle, WA 98101
(206) 382-3587 • fax: (206) 292-9890
website: http://members.aol.com/edapinc

EDAP is dedicated to promoting the awareness and prevention of eating disorders by encouraging positive self-esteem and size acceptance. It provides free and low-cost educational information on eating disorders and their prevention. EDAP also provides educational outreach programs and training for schools and universities and sponsors the Puppet Project for Schools and the annual National Eating Disorders Awareness Week. EDAP publishes a prevention curriculum for grades four through six as well as public prevention and awareness information packets, videos, guides, and other materials.

**Harvard Eating Disorders Center (HEDC)**
356 Boylston St., Boston, MA 02118
(888) 236-1188

HEDC is a national nonprofit organization dedicated to research and education. It works to expand knowledge about eating disorders and their detection, treatment, and prevention and promotes the healthy development of women, children, and everyone at risk. A primary goal for the organization is lobbying for health policy initiatives on behalf of individuals with eating disorders.

### National Association of Anorexia and Associated Disorders (ANAD)
Box 7, Highland Park, IL 60035
(847) 831-3438 • hot line: (847) 831-3438 • fax: (847) 433-4632
e-mail: anad20@aol.com
website: http://members.aol.com/anad20/

ANAD offers hot-line counseling, operates an international network of support groups for people with eating disorders and their families, and provides referrals to health care professionals who treat eating disorders. It produces a quarterly newsletter and information packets and organizes national conferences and local programs. All ANAD services are provided free of charge.

### National Eating Disorder Information Centre (NEDIC)
CW 1–211, 200 Elizabeth St., Toronto, ON M5G 2C4, Canada
(416) 340-4156 • fax: (416) 340-4736
e-mail: mbeck@torhosp.toronto.on.ca • website: www.nedic.on.ca

NEDIC provides information and resources on eating disorders and weight preoccupation, and it focuses on the socio-cultural factors that influence female health-related behaviors. NEDIC promotes healthy lifestyles and encourages individuals to make informed choices based on accurate information. It publishes a newsletter and a guide for families and friends of eating-disorder sufferers and sponsors Eating Disorders Awareness Week in Canada.

### National Eating Disorders Organization (NEDO)
6655 S. Yale Ave., Tulsa, OK 74136
(918) 481-4044
website: www.laureate.com

NEDO provides information, prevention, and treatment resources for all forms of eating disorders. It believes that eating disorders are multidimensional, developed and sustained by biological, social, psychological, and familial factors. It publishes information packets, a video, and a newsletter, and it holds a semi-annual national conference.

# Bibliography of Books

Suzanne Abraham and Derek Llewellyn-Jones — *Eating Disorders: The Facts*. Oxford: Oxford University Press, 1997.

Jean Antonello — *Breaking Out of Food Jail: How to Free Yourself from Diets and Problem Eating Once and for All*. New York: Simon & Schuster, 1996.

Marianne Apostolides — *Inner Hunger: A Young Woman's Struggle Through Anorexia and Bulimia*. New York: W.W. Norton, 1998.

Frances M. Berg — *Afraid to Eat: Children and Teens in Weight Crisis*. Hettinger, ND: Healthy Weight Journal, 1997.

Susan Bordo — *Unbearable Weight: Feminism, Western Culture, and the Body*. Berkeley: University of California Press, 1993.

Hilde Bruch — *The Golden Cage—The Enigma of Anorexia Nervosa*. New York: Vintage, 1979.

Joan Jacobs Brumberg — *Fasting Girls: The History of Anorexia Nervosa*. New York: Penguin Books, 1988.

Kim Chernin — *The Hungry Self: Women, Eating, and Identity*. New York: Times Books, 1985.

Kim Chernin — *The Obsession: Reflections on the Tyranny of Slenderness*. New York: Harper & Row, 1981.

Peggy Claude-Pierre — *The Secret Language of Eating Disorders: The Revolutionary New Approach to Understanding and Curing Anorexia and Bulimia*. New York: Times Books, 1997.

Carolyn Costin — *Your Dieting Daughter: Is She Dying for Attention?* New York: Brunner/Mazel, 1997.

Ophira Edut, ed. — *Adios, Barbie: Young Women Write About Body Image and Identity*. Seattle: Seal Press, 1998.

Laura Fraser — *Losing It: America's Obsession with Weight and the Industry That Feeds on It*. New York: Dutton, 1997.

Nan Kathryn Fuchs — *Overcoming the Legacy of Overeating: How to Change Your Negative Eating Habits*. Los Angeles: Lowell House, 1996.

W. Charisse Goodman — *The Invisible Woman: Confronting Weight Prejudice in America*. Carlsbad, CA: Gurze Books, 1995.

Heather M. Gray and Samantha Phillips — *Real Girl/Real World: Tools for Finding Your True Self*. Seattle: Seal Press, 1998.

Rosemary Green — *Diary of a Fat Housewife*. New York: Warner Books, 1996.

Sharlene Hesse-Biber — *Am I Thin Enough Yet? The Cult of Thinness and the Commercialization of Identity*. Oxford: Oxford University Press, 1996.

Marya Hornbacher — *Wasted: A Memoir of Anorexia and Bulimia*. New York: HarperCollins, 1998.

Michael Krasnow — *My Life as a Male Anorexic*. New York: Harrington Park Press, 1996.

Marilyn Lawrence, ed. — *Fed Up and Hungry: Women, Oppression, and Food*. London: Women's Press, 1987.

Steven Levenkron — *Treating and Overcoming Anorexia Nervosa*. New York: Warner Books, 1997.

Morag MacSween — *Anorexic Bodies: A Feminist and Sociological Perspective on Anorexia Nervosa*. New York: Routledge, 1993.

Helen Malson — *The Thin Woman*. New York: Routledge, 1998.

Carol Emery Normandi and Laurelee Roark — *It's Not About Food*. New York: Penguin, 1998.

Susie Orbach — *Fat Is a Feminist Issue: The Anti-Diet Guide for Women*. New York: Galahad Books, 1997.

Mary Bray Pipher — *Hunger Pains: The Modern Woman's Tragic Quest for Thinness*. New York: Ballantine Books, 1997.

Brett Silverstein and Deborah Perlick — *The Cost of Competence: Why Inequality Causes Depression, Eating Disorders, and Illness in Women*. Oxford: Oxford University Press, 1995.

Becky W. Thompson — *A Hunger So Wide and So Deep*. Minneapolis: University of Minnesota Press, 1994.

L.M. Vincent — *Competing with the Sylph*. New York: Berkeley Books, 1979.

Naomi Wolf — *The Beauty Myth*. Toronto: Vintage Press, 1990.

Kathryn J. Zerbe — *The Body Betrayed: A Deeper Understanding of Women, Eating Disorders, and Treatment*. Carlsbad, CA: Gurze Books, 1995.

# Index

Abraham, Suzanne, 40
adolescents
  are at risk for eating disorders, 40–49
    dieting increases, 108
    early puberty increases, 51–52
    eating behavior among, 44–46
    parents can influence, 160–61
    hormonal changes in, 42–43
    perception of body shape and size
      among
    media influence on, 41–42
Agras, W. Stewart, 13, 57
alcohol abuse. *See* substance abuse
American Medical Association
  on ideal body weight, 26
American Psychological Association,
  129
Anderson, Arnold E., 74
anorexia nervosa
  from activity, 61
  in adults, 54–55
  deaths from, 21, 122, 134
    are exaggerated, 22, 23
  definition of, 12
  genetic, personality, and biological
    contributions to, 55–57
  increase in rate of, 18
  midlife triggers of, 56
  side effects of, 27, 67
  treatment, 57–58
    cost of, 127
    hospitalization, 125–32
    obstacles to, 114
    patients should be allowed to
      refuse, 133–38
*Archives of Pediatric and Adolescent
Medicine* (journal), 19
Aspaas, Kenneth, 127

Baenenm, Judith, 160
ballet
  anorexia among dancers, 65
*Beauty Myth: How Images of Beauty Are
  Used Against Women* (Wolf), 22
Becker, Anne, 12, 79, 81
Beron, Elizabeth, 71
Berzins, Lisa, 151
Binks, Georgie, 31
body image
  among adolescents, 43–44
    media influence on, 41–42
  connection with illness, 81
  cultural influences on, 41
  problems with, can start in grade
    school, 50–51

Body Image, Food, and Self-Esteem
  program, 148–49
Body Image Summit, 141
body weight
  as diagnostic criteria for eating
    disorders, 64
  ideal, 26
Brumberg, Joan, 22
Bulik, Cynthia, 14
bulimia nervosa
  characteristic behavior in, 94
  as coping mechanism, 95–96
  deaths from, 23
  definition of, 12–13, 27
  and dieting, 110
  pharmacological treatment of,
    118–20
  recovery from, 111
  side effects of, 28–29, 88

Caron, Ann, 161
Carpenter, Karen, 89
Casey, John, 82
Center for Science in the Public
  Interest, 156
Chernin, Kim, 63
Cherry, Susan Spaeth, 158
Chodorow, Nancy, 95
Chrisler, Joan, 51
Concerned Counseling, 108
Cook, Christine, 67, 68
Crenson, Matt, 14
culture
  Fijian
    and eating disorders, 12, 79–81
  impact on body image, 103–106

DeMarco, Donald, 21
DeNoon, Daniel J., 118
depression, 13–14, 118
Despres, Renée, 59
Dexfenfluramine, 117
diabetes, 51
Diana, Princess, 89
dieting
  can cause eating disorders, 100–11,
    128–29
  industry
    legislation is needed to control, 156
    preys on dieters' desperation, 153
    size of, 101
  myths about, 153–54
  prevalence of, among adolescents, 44,
    46–47
*Don't Stop Loving Me: A Reassuring*

*Guide for Mothers of Adolescent Daughters* (Caron), 161
Draper, Heather, 114, 133
drug abuse. *See* substance abuse
drugs, pharmacological, 115–20
Dunn, Thomas, 23

eating
  among adolescents, 44–46
    parents can influence, 160–61
  compulsive, 108–109
  effects of neurotransmitters on, 116
Eating Attitudes Test, 89
eating disorders
  age of onset, 47, 48, 102, 159
  are not necessarily harmful, 31–36
    con, 25–30
  at-risk groups for
    adolescent girls, 40–48
    adult women, 53–58
    ballet dancers, 65
    female athletes, 59–68
      warning signs in, 64–65
    men, 69–74
    preteens, 49–52
  body weight as diagnostic criteria for, 64
  deaths from, 21, 122, 134
    are exaggerated, 22, 23
  long-term effects of, 29–30
  male-female ratio in, 71
  prevalence of, 26, 32
    among adolescents, 45–46, 50
    among men, 70–71
    anorexia vs. bulimia, 88
    is overstated, 21–24
      con, 17–20
    in United Kingdom, 83
  and serotonin, link between, 116–17
  side effects of, 51, 122
  sports environments can foster, 61–63
  *see also* anorexia nervosa; bulimia nervosa; treatment
*Eating Disorders, Body Image, and the Media* (British Media Association), 82, 83
*Eating Disorders* (Hsu), 102
"Eating Disorders in Males: Critical Questions" (Anderson), 74
*Eating Disorders: The Facts* (Abraham and Llewellyn-Jones), 40
education
  benefits of, 143–44
  can help in prevention of eating disorders, 142–45
  contacts for resources, 145
  may increase incidence of eating disorders, 146–50
  school-based, 144
Eller, Daryn, 49

family
  attitudes of
    contribute to development of eating disorders, 87–99
  therapy
    in treatment of eating disorders, 123–24
*Fasting Girls: The Emergence of Anorexia Nervosa as a Modern Disease* (Brumberg), 22
fathers
  influence of, on eating disorders, 77, 92–93, 98–99
"female athlete triad," 39
Fenfluramine, 120
Fiji
  arrival of television and eating disorders on, 12, 79–81
Fleming, Barbara, 50
Fluoxetine, 119
Fluvoxamine, 119
Fonda, Jane, 89
Fontenot, Beth, 23
*Food Insight* (magazine), 93
France, David, 133
Friedman, Michelle, 52
Fulkerson, Katherine, 60, 61, 64, 68
Fuller, William, 127

Gilbert, Stefanie, 160
Girl Power campaign, 156
*Glamour* (magazine)
  surveys
    on body image, 104
    on treatment under managed care, 128
Glazier, Sheri, 54, 57
Goldstein, Robin, 161
Goodman, Ellen, 78
Goodwin, Renee, 77
government
  role of, in prevention of eating disorders, 151–57
Graber, Julia A., 50, 52
Grady, Denise, 146
Greenberg, Pamela, 130
Guenther, Heidi, 39

Halmi, Katherine A., 123, 128, 130, 149
Hamilton, Linda, 39
Harrison, Marvel, 63, 64
*Harvard Mental Health Letter*, 12, 14, 137

Health and Human Services
    Department, U.S.
    Girl Power campaign of, 156
*Health Psychology* (journal), 147
Hesse-Biber, Sharlene, 87
Hopper, Mary, 55
Hornbacher, Marya, 28
Howard, W.T., 130
Hsu, L.K. George, 102
Hughes, Nikki, 134
Hunter, Rita, 85

*International Journal of Eating Disorders,*
    18, 103
*Irish Times* (newspaper), 85
*It's Not About Food* (Normandi and
    Roark), 100

Jones, Liz, 141
Jones-Hicks, Linda, 52
*Journal of Consulting and Clinical
    Psychology,* 20
*Journal of the American Dietetic
    Association,* 102

Kaye, Walter, 130
Kendall, Samantha, 134
Klein, Sarah, 25
*Knowledge Explosion: Generations of
    Feminist Scholarship,* 22
Koudsi, Suzanne, 69

Landers, Ann, 22
Litynski, Diane, 56
Llewellyn-Jones, Derek, 40

Maloney, Danielle, 144
managed care
    organizations often deny treatment,
        128–30
Mann, Tracy, 147, 148, 149
Mattingly, Kate, 65
media
    contribute to incidence of eating
        disorders, 78–81
        con, 82–86
    girls need education to combat
        effects of, 155–56
    and perception of body shape, 41–42
Medical Sciences Bulletin, 115
Mee, Cynthia, 160
Meehan, Vivian Hanson, 128
men
    are at risk for eating disorders, 69–74
    are victims of discrimination, 24
    with eating disorders
        categories of, 72–74
        clinical features of, 118

menstruation
    disruption of, 27
    as warning sign, 64–65
    and eating behavior, 44
Mental Health Act (Great Britain), 136
Moore, Striegel, 152
Mosely, Benita Fitzgerald, 39
mothers
    attitudes of, influence daughters,
        96–98

Nathanson, Bernard, 24
Nathanson, Vivienne, 83, 86
National Association of Anorexia
    Nervosa and Associated Disorders,
        70, 128
    on age of onset of eating disorders,
        102, 159
    on prevalence of eating disorders, 32
National Center for Health Statistics
    on deaths from anorexia, 23
National Institute of Mental Health
    on deaths from anorexia, 122
    on prevalence of eating disorders
        among adolescents, 50
National Women's Health Information
    Center, 125
*Never Too Thin* (Seid), 102
Normandi, Carol Emery, 100

obesity
    as chronic medical condition, 116
    prevalence of, 16, 19–20
O'Dea, Jennifer, 144
Olivardia, Roberto, 70, 72, 74
Osborn, Lawrence, 131
Overholser, Geneva, 16

parents
    role of, in prevention of eating
        disorders, 158–61
*Pediatrics* (journal), 19
Polsenberg, Caroline, 57
Pope, Harrison G., 71, 72
Poppink, Joanna, 142
prevention
    educational programs
        can help, 142–45
        may increase incidence, 146–50
    role of
        government in, 151–57
        parents in, 158–61
Prozac, 116, 129
psychologists
    role of, in treatment of eating
        disorders, 122–23
*Psychotherapy Letter,* 73

Renes, Susan, 19
Renter, Tammy, 126, 127, 131
*Revolution Within: A Book of Self-
Esteem, The* (Steinem), 22
*Riverside Health NHS v. Fox*, 135
Roark, Laurelee, 100
Rodin, Judith, 16
Roselin, Joel M., 56
Rosenthal, Elaine, 29
Russell, Janice, 114

Sacker, Ira, 71, 72, 74
Seid, Roberta, 102
selective serotonin-reuptake inhibitors
(SSRIs), 115
in treatment of bulimia, 119–20
self-image
impact of media on, 18–19, 159
Sell, Betsy, 127
serotonin
link with eating disorders, 116–17
*Seventeen* (magazine), 13
Shulman, Alexandra, 141
Smith, Joan, 12
Stacey, Michelle, 149
starvation
effects of, 34, 67
Steinem, Gloria, 22
Stice, Eric, 13
*Stop Treating Me Like a Kid* (Goldstein),
161
Strober, Michael, 127
substance abuse
among bulimics, 29
and cultural pressures on women,
106
surveys
on body image, 104
among adolescents, 44–46
of doctors, on treatment under
managed care, 128, 129
on eating behavior, among
adolescents, 44
on weight control measures, 46–48

Tanner, Dave, 67
Taylor, C. Barr, 150
therapy, cognitive
in treatment of eating disorders, 123
Thibeault, Suzi, 65
thyroid
effects of anorexia on, 27
Trazodone, 120
treatment
hospitalization, 125–32
obstacles to, 114
with pharmacological drugs, 115–20
with psychotherapy, 121–24
Tuttle, Amy, 93

*U.S. News & World Report* (magazine),
101

Vreeland, Leslie, 53

Walsh, B. Timothy, 54, 57
*Washington Post* (newspaper), 16
*Wasted: A Memoir of Anorexia and
Bulimia*, 149
weight-loss industry. *See* dieting,
industry
Weintraub, Robert, 116
Welzel, Jane, 61, 62
Wheeler, Brooke C., 17
Wolf, Naomi, 22, 23
women
at risk for eating disorders, 53–58
adult, 53–58
athletes, 59–68
cultural pressures on, 105–106
*Women's Sports & Fitness* (magazine), 59
Wurtman, Judith and Richard, 116,
117

Yarborough, Kathryn Putnam, 13

Zimmerman, Jill S., 80
Zofran, 118